Berried Alive

Berried Alive

Kate Kingsbury

WHEELER
CHIVERS

This Large Print edition is published by Wheeler Publishing, Waterville, Maine USA and by BBC Audiobooks, Ltd, Bath, England.

Published in 2004 in the U.S. by arrangement with The Berkley Publishing Group, a division of Penguin Group (USA) Inc.

Published in 2005 in the U.K. by arrangement with the author.

U.S. Hardcover 1-58724-791-7 (Cozy Mystery)
U.K. Hardcover 1-4056-3177-5 (Chivers Large Print)
U.K. Softcover 1-4056-3178-3 (Camden Large Print)

This is a work of fiction. Names, characters, places, and incidents either are the product of the author's imagination or are used fictitiously, and any resemblance to actual persons, living or dead, business establishments, events, or locales is entirely coincidental.

The text of this Large Print edition is unabridged.
Other aspects of the book may vary from the original edition.

Set in 16 pt. Plantin by Christina S. Huff.

Printed in the United States on permanent paper.

British Library Cataloguing-in-Publication Data available

Library of Congress Cataloging-in-Publication Data

Kingsbury, Kate.
    Berried alive / Kate Kingsbury.
        p. cm.
    ISBN 1-58724-791-7 (lg. print : sc : alk. paper)
    1. World War, 1939–1945 — England — Fiction.   2. Women detectives — England — Fiction.   3. Soldiers — Crimes against — Fiction.   4. Americans — England — Fiction.   5. Villages — Fiction.   6. Manors — Fiction.   I. Title.
PR9199.3.K44228B47 2004
813'.6—dc22   2004054214

Berried Alive

Chapter 1

It all began with Martin's spectacles. Or, to be more precise, the absence of them.

Lady Elizabeth Hartleigh Compton had been late in rising that morning, thanks to a restless night filled with disturbing dreams. She was not in the mood to deal with one of Violet's tantrums.

Her volatile housekeeper was in a tizzy, as usual, about Martin's lack of common sense. Since Martin had long ago exhausted his capabilities as a butler in the vast Manor House and was fast approaching senility, it seemed to Elizabeth that to expect any amount of sense from his addled brain was being somewhat optimistic.

Martin had his moments, true, but by and large he was more a responsibility than an asset. Violet was well aware of that and had agreed to overlook the old gentleman's shortcomings. Indeed, both she and Elizabeth went to great pains to assure Martin he was still in complete control of his faculties — not an easy task at times. Then again, nothing in these war-torn times was simple anymore. Which was why Elizabeth felt that Violet overreacted when Martin wandered into the kitchen that morning wearing his customary vague expression.

It had taken Elizabeth a moment or two to realize why he looked different. Violet had her back to him at first, and hadn't noticed that anything was amiss. Elizabeth stared at him, while he stared back at her, seemingly unaware that she was scrutinizing him.

"It's your glasses!" Elizabeth snapped her fingers in her butler's face, making him sway backward in alarm. "That's what's wrong."

Violet, busily stirring something at the stove, demanded without turning around, "What's wrong with his glasses? Don't tell me he broke them."

"Well, he's not wearing them." Elizabeth reached out a soothing hand and patted Martin's shoulder. "It's all right, Martin. You probably forgot to put them on this morning, didn't you?"

Martin stared down at his legs in dismay. "Good Lord! I did?" He shook his head. "You must be mistaken. I appear to be properly attired."

"Not your trousers," Elizabeth said patiently. "Your glasses." She tapped his wrinkled forehead. "They're not there." She had to smile. She was so used to seeing the gold-rimmed specs perched on the end of his nose. Although he never looked through them, preferring to peer over the top of them, they had been an integral part of his face for as long as she could remember. Without them he looked rather like an aging goldfish with eyebrows.

Violet spun around, the wooden spoon in her hand shedding tiny bits of the mess she liked to call scrambled eggs. Lacking the real thing, the housekeeper was forced to use dried egg mixed with milk for Sunday breakfast. While Elizabeth valiantly declared the result every bit as good as real eggs, Martin had no compunction in denouncing the rubbery concoction an insult and a threat to his digestive system. Violet's harsh reminders that there was a war on and they had to make sacrifices fell on deaf ears. Martin grumbled with every mouthful.

"What the blue blazes did you do with them?" she demanded, glaring at poor Martin as if he had committed a mortal sin. "You only have two places to put them — your dresser and your nose. Surely you could manage to find one of them without buggering it up."

Martin's frail hand wandered to his nose. "Glasses? Where are they? I'm sure I had them on this morning. I distinctly remember greeting the master in the great hall, and I know I had them on then."

Violet's eyeballs rolled up toward the ceiling. "Here he goes again." She waved her spoon at him. "How many times do I have to tell you, you silly old goat. The master is dead. One of Hitler's bombs got him in the Blitz. Him and madam. They're both dead as doornails, so you

9

couldn't have seen either one of them." She glanced at Elizabeth. "Sorry, Lizzie."

Elizabeth nodded affably. Saddened as she had been to lose both her parents in a bombing raid, she had learned to accept Violet's somewhat blasé references to their demise in the spirit they were uttered — not as a demonstration of disrespect, but as an earnest endeavor to convince Martin of their passing. The fact that Martin stubbornly insisted he not only saw Elizabeth's father, but chatted almost daily with the late Lord Wellsborough, did nothing to deter Violet from her appointed task.

Violet, in fact, enjoyed a unique position in the late earl of Wellsborough's household. Normally, any such familiarity with the mistress of the Manor House would not have been tolerated from a lowly housekeeper. But the Second World War, the changing times, and Elizabeth's fondness for the woman who had been a part of the household since her childhood, eliminated old-fashioned proprieties and Violet was allowed indiscretions that would have caused Elizabeth's parents to roll over in their graves.

Right now, she stood frowning at Elizabeth, while the yellow mess continued to drip from her spoon. "I don't know what he'll be up to next. Proper nitwit, he is. He's probably left them on the dresser. I'll have to send Sadie to look in his room. She's cleaning the bathrooms, but she'll be finished soon."

Reluctant to divert the housemaid from her

appointed tasks, Elizabeth shook her head. "Never mind. I'll have Polly look for them this morning. It's not as if he needs them." She drew out a chair from the table and sat down.

Martin hovered at her side for a moment then said a trifle pompously, "May I have the pleasure of joining you at the table, madam?"

"You may, Martin."

"Thank you, madam."

She watched him drag a chair sideways, then lower his creaking bones onto it. Finding that he was facing away from the table, he tutted irritably, got painfully to his feet, twisted the chair toward the table, then squeezed into the narrow space he'd left himself. Thus seated, he lifted his hand and scratched his nose.

Guessing what was coming, Elizabeth waited.

A dazed expression crept over Martin's face. "Great Scott," he muttered. "Someone has stolen my glasses. No doubt it's one of those damn Americans. Pardon my impertinence, madam, but I did warn you that there would be trouble if you allowed those savages the run of the manor."

Elizabeth's tolerance vanished. In view of Martin's advanced age, she often made allowances for him, but one thing she would not stand was any derogatory comments about the American airmen billeted in the manor. "Martin," she said tartly, "our American guests are not savages. They are extremely courageous men sacrificing their lives to help fight our war and save our country. The very least we can do is offer them our hospitality. We owe them so much more than that."

"I don't remember you offering them hospitality," Violet said over her shoulder. She had turned back to the stove and couldn't see Elizabeth's expression. "I seem to remember the war office demanding that we put up with them."

"I didn't hear you complaining when Major Monroe brought you all those extra rations from the airbase."

"Oh, so that's what's got you all ruffled up this morning." Violet turned, a steaming plate in each hand. "You're pining for that major, that's what."

Elizabeth gritted her teeth. "I'm not pining for anyone, Violet, and please refrain from inferring that there's anything personal in my relationship with Earl Monroe."

Violet dumped a plate in front of her. "Just saying what I see, that's all. You can argue until you're blue in the face about it, but I know what's what between you two. I've seen the way he looks at you, and how you get all in a dither whenever he's around. Never was like that with your Harry. Not that I can blame you. Always knew Harry was no good. I don't know why you married him in the first place, and that's a fact."

"Not that it's any of your business, but for want of a better reason, I suppose I was young and silly." Elizabeth stared in distaste at the grayish yellow mound on her plate. Even the addition of fried tomatoes and mushrooms failed to make the dish look appetizing.

"Right, and look where it got you. Lost your entire inheritance because of his gambling. If you hadn't divorced him when you did you'd have lost the Manor House as well."

"That might still happen if we don't get some of the bills paid soon."

"If you'll pardon me for saying so, madam," Martin said, blinking owlishly at her with watery eyes, "arguing at the table can cause serious problems with your digestion."

"Quite right, Martin." Elizabeth picked up her knife and fork. "I think we've had enough of this conversation."

"Where's the major been, anyway?" Violet carried a third plate to the table and sat down. "Have you heard from him lately?"

"No, I haven't." Elizabeth chewed on a mouthful of the eggs and swallowed it down. "Nor am I expecting the military to inform me of the major's whereabouts so there's no point in asking."

"All right, no need to get uppity about it. I was just wondering if any of the other lads had mentioned where he might be. Not like him to stay away without a word as to when he'd be back. I hope he isn't poorly like those Yanks who died. Four of them, the paper said. All of them died of the same thing and none of the doctors know what they died of. Blinking scary if you ask me."

"I'm not aware that anyone asked you anything," Martin mumbled.

Elizabeth gave up trying to avoid the subject. "I think we'd know if the major was ill. After all, his quarters are here in the east wing. Someone would have let us know. I imagine he's on a mission. You know very well the men are not allowed to talk about missions."

The ominous silence that followed her comment sent a chill through her bones.

"Well," Violet said at last, in a voice that was obviously meant to sound reassuring, "I'm sure we'll be hearing from him before too long."

That was the problem, Elizabeth thought, as she nudged some tomato onto her fork, no one could be sure of anything. Although Earl made a point of avoiding any real discussion of the missions he flew, Elizabeth was painfully aware of the dangers. If anything happened to him, she knew without a doubt that her world would never be the same again.

It didn't seem to matter that such thoughts were forbidden, never to be voiced. Major Earl Monroe was married and had a family waiting for him back home in America. She had long ago stopped obsessing about her guilt, however. She couldn't help her feelings, and as long as she kept them to herself, she could see no harm in indulging in a fantasy now and again. Though lately the fantasies had become a trifle risqué to be dwelling in the mind of a lady.

Martin interrupted with a snort that startled

her out of her thoughts. "It's not proper. That's what I say."

Violet raised her skimpy eyebrows. "What's not proper?"

Elizabeth stared at him in apprehension, wondering wildly if he somehow acquired the ability to read her thoughts.

"It's not proper that madam eats here at the kitchen table with the servants. I know the master would be most displeased if he were to catch us like this."

"The master's not going to catch anything, you blubbering fool," Violet said, raising her voice. "Not unless he can fit all the blown-up pieces of himself together again and climb up out of the earth."

This was a bit much, even for Elizabeth. "I think I'll take the dogs for a walk," she announced, pushing her chair back from the table. "It's a lovely day out there. They'll enjoy a run along the cliffs."

"Too bad you can't take them on the beach." Violet scraped the last of her eggs onto her fork.

Martin looked up. "That's a marvelous idea. A walk on the beach would be very nice."

"You can't walk on the beach, can you, nincompoop." Violet glared at him. "It's mined, isn't it. One wrong step and you'll be in as many pieces as the master."

Martin glared back. "I have no intention of walking on the beach. I was, however, rather hoping that you would."

"Well, I'll be blowed." Violet bristled, her gray frizzy hair seeming to stand on end. "Of all the sauce."

Elizabeth left them to their argument, secure in the knowledge that disagreement had become something of a sport between her butler and her housekeeper, each trying to outdo the other with their insults. Normally she tolerated their spats, and sometimes even enjoyed them, but right now she was in no mood for it.

It had been over a week since she had seen or heard from Earl, and she was more than a little concerned. News of the outbreak of a deadly illness that had already taken the lives of four Americans on the base only compounded her fears for his safety. The last time she'd seen him he'd hinted at an important campaign in the near future, but she had expected more warning than a vague hint.

Not that she had any right to be notified of his every move, she reminded herself, as she watched the dogs chase each other across the rough grass. It was just that he normally let her know if he was going to be away for any length of time, and she was rather peeved that he hadn't done so this time.

It was such a beautiful morning. How she would have loved to share it with the man she secretly adored. The fresh salty breeze from the ocean tugged at her carefully pinned hair, threatening to dislodge the French twist.

Beneath her feet, warmed by the sun, bell

heather and clumps of fragrant clover mingled with the smell of sand and seaweed. Another summer was beginning, another year half over. How many more would the world have to endure before this dreadful war dragged to an end?

She shaded her eyes to stare out to sea, where the sparkle of sunlight on the placid waves was bright enough to dazzle her. Just above the horizon she could see a smudge of dark cloud. Or perhaps it was a squadron returning from yet another dangerous raid on Germany.

Was Earl up there in that brilliant blue sky, flying above the ocean with his sights firmly fixed on the welcoming shores of England? Or was he trapped somewhere over there, perhaps injured, perhaps captured, helpless in the clutches of a ruthless enemy?

The thought was so horrifying she almost lost her balance. Determined not to dwell on such macabre thoughts, she turned her back on the encroaching ocean and scanned the cliffs for the dogs. George and Gracie, a gift from Earl and named after stars of an American radio show, were some distance away, bounding across the grass toward someone walking rapidly to meet them.

It was as if her heart suddenly soared far above the sparkling water and hovered there, afraid to answer to the hope pounding in her chest.

The dogs' joyful barks of welcome floated across the grassy slopes and she knew then, that

17

her prayers had been answered. Unmindful of the tears wetting her cheeks, she raced after the dogs, stumbling now and then on the uneven ground. He was here, and he was in one piece. *Thank God! Oh, thank God!*

Heart pounding, she galloped toward the man greeting the enthusiastic dogs. He had never looked more handsome, standing tall in the forest green uniform, his light brown hair ruffled by the wind, ice blue eyes laughing at her as she reached him, his mouth curved in a boyish grin that melted away every dark thought in her mind.

She had to muster every ounce of her composure to refrain from flinging her arms around his neck and holding on tight enough to strangle him. Her breath destroyed, more from the excitement and relief of seeing him again than her mad dash across the cliffs, she could only grin foolishly back at him.

"Elizabeth. It's good to see you."

His deep voice seemed to flow into her veins, carrying warmth throughout her entire body. She managed to sound fairly coherent when she answered him. "It's awfully good to see you, too."

For a long moment he just stood there staring into her eyes, while she gazed helplessly into his, shaken by her desperate yearning to touch him. When he finally spoke, the words were so mundane she almost laughed. "So, how have you been?"

The spell broken, she did her best to come back down to earth. "Incredibly busy. And you?"

He bent over to pat the dogs, who were shoving each other out of the way to nudge his legs with their noses. "Things have been a little interesting lately. Seems to have quieted now, though."

And that was most likely all she would ever hear of whatever horrors he'd been through in the past week. "We were rather afraid you'd caught that awful illness going around the base," she said, as he straightened again. "Violet was most concerned."

His gaze seemed to penetrate her soul. "Only Violet?"

Aware that he was teasing her, she muddled her words. "No, of course not. I mean, we were all concerned. *I* was concerned. Of course. We . . . I . . . we all were worried about you."

To her extreme joy and confusion, he linked her arm through his and began leading her across the grass toward the ocean. Her expression must have betrayed her emotion, as he added lightly, "Is this permitted, your ladyship?"

She was tempted to tell him that right at that moment she wouldn't have cared if they were lying naked on the grass together. Appalled by her thoughts, she said quickly, "There's no one to see us. We seem to be quite alone out here this morning."

"Just making sure. I wouldn't want your loyal subjects to think I was taking advantage of you."

She wrinkled her nose at him. "You make me sound impossibly snobbish."

He laughed. "Sorry. I guess I'll never understand the British devotion to protocol."

"That's all right. We don't expect you to understand any more than we understand the Americans' lack of it."

"Ouch." She felt his gaze on her face. "Is something bothering you, Elizabeth?"

She paused before answering, afraid she would blurt out what was on her mind. *Everything* was bothering her: The fact that she had no right to ask him where he'd been this past week; the fact that she wasn't free to express the passion she felt for him; the fact that she was forced to contain her desire to hug him, kiss him and whatever delicious events might follow after that.

It wasn't just his marriage that stood in the way, though that was a huge part of it. It was her standing as lady of the manor, the respected guardian of the village of Sitting Marsh, that prevented her from enjoying such simple pleasures as holding his hand, or basking in the warmth of his arms.

"What is it?" He paused, dropping her arm to turn to her, his face creased in a frown.

Feeling suddenly bereft without the warm pressure of his hand, she said quickly, "Oh, it's nothing. I was just a little concerned about the illness that has struck the base. Is it as bad as the rumors make it sound?"

Shoving his hands in his pockets, he stared out at the restless ocean. "Four guys have died so far. That's all I know. The medics are working around the clock trying to figure out what killed them."

"Well, I hope they find out before it spreads to the village."

"Elizabeth, if I tell you something, will you promise to keep it to yourself?"

"Well, of course." A chill touched her spine at his worried expression. "Is it worse than we thought? Is there likely to be an epidemic?"

"No, I don't think so." He seemed to wrestle with his thoughts for a moment then said quietly, "The four guys who died. They all had something in common."

Puzzled, she frowned at him. "You mean the same symptoms?"

"Well, that too . . ." He sighed. "All four men had red hair."

Her eyes widened, wondering for a brief instant if he was teasing her again. "Red hair?"

He nodded, his gaze watchful on her face. "What does that suggest to you?"

Now she understood. "It suggests," she said slowly, "that either the mysterious ailment is particularly selective, or someone has an intense dislike of male redheads."

"Right." Earl's mouth tightened. "The medics think they were poisoned."

"Oh, dear." Elizabeth's hand strayed to her throat. "It seems all too much of a coincidence, doesn't it."

"Well, it's all theory right now." Earl whistled to the dogs, and squatted on his heels as they hurled themselves toward him. "The last I heard they were waiting for some lab tests to come back."

"Did the men who died have anything else in common? Besides the red hair, I mean."

He looked up at her, a frown creasing his brow. "Yeah, they did. Every one of them spent their last evening on earth at the Tudor Arms."

Chills raced down Elizabeth's spine. Resentment of the Americans was rife in the village, and she was in constant dread that one day the hostility would erupt into something very dangerous. It appeared that maybe her worst fears were about to be realized.

Chapter 2

"I find it hard to believe," Elizabeth said slowly, "that someone at the Tudor Arms poisoned four men."

"If it *is* poison." Earl got to his feet, brushing dog hairs from his sharply creased pants. "Guess we won't know that for sure until the lab tests come back."

"Do you know which night the men were down there?"

"Apparently they were there on different nights."

"Then doesn't it seem more likely they were poisoned by something on the base?"

"It's possible, I guess."

"But you don't think so."

His expression was grave. "I don't know what to think."

"I suppose it's futile to hope that it's simply a case of food poisoning?"

"Not likely. If it was something in the food, spread over a week or more, you'd figure on a lot more people being affected by it. No one else on the base is sick. Not like that, anyway. Have you heard of anyone in the village being sick the last week or two?"

"No, I haven't. Certainly not a fatal illness, anyway. I'm quite sure I would have heard about that." She paused, tilting her head on one side to look up at him. "I can make a few inquiries, if you like?"

"I'm always afraid to ask you to do that. You have a lousy habit of getting into trouble when you start asking questions."

She grinned at him. "But you need my help, right?"

"Right." He sighed. "You know how tough it is for our guys to get anything out of the village folks. They'll talk to you. Besides, you're darn good at ferreting out anything suspicious. Not like those chumps at the local constabulary. I wouldn't trust them to solve a jigsaw puzzle."

His praise made her light-headed. "George and Sid mean well," she murmured. "But after being retired for so long, it's hard for them to get back to being policemen again. Especially since they were more or less forced into it. That's the problem with wars, they take away all the able-bodied men."

"Seems to me the women are doing a pretty good job of filling in for them." He whistled to the dogs, who were wandering just a little too close to the cliff edge. "Maybe they should put your friend . . . what's her name . . . Rita Crumm in charge of the constables. She could get them licked into shape in no time."

Although she knew he was joking, Elizabeth gasped in horror. "A woman constable? Never!

24

And Rita? Heaven forbid. She'd have everyone in prison before the week was out. And she's not my friend, by the way. Far from it. I put up with her because I have to, but there's certainly no love lost between us."

Earl laughed. "That's a pretty big understatement. From what I've seen of you two, I figure you'd like to tear each other apart."

"At times, I suppose. It's just that Rita is under the mistaken impression that she's in charge of the war effort in Sitting Marsh, thereby giving her the right to order everyone about as if they were her slaves. That ridiculous Housewives League, for instance. It's just an excuse for Rita to lord it over everyone."

"Everyone but you." He linked her arm through his again. "No one lords it over the lady of the manor."

She peeked up at him. "Are you making fun of me?"

"Never." He hugged her arm to his side. "Now tell me what's been happening at the manor while I've been gone."

Happily she did as he asked. She told him about Polly, her juvenile assistant, and the young girl's latest attempts to reunite with her GI boyfriend, and Sadie's bizarre methods of dealing with her housemaid duties.

She told him about Violet's disastrous experiments with rationed ingredients in her baking, which never had been too inspiring anyway, and about Martin's lost spectacles. Mentioning them reminded her that she would have to ask Polly to look for them.

All the time she was conscious of the blissful moments slipping away, and the knowledge that soon Earl would be gone again, and once more she would be terrified for his safety until he returned.

Rita Crumm glared at the women crammed together in her sparse front room. Not one of them was paying any attention to her. If there was one thing Rita could not abide, it was being ignored. Especially by that loudmouth, Marge Gunther, whose voice sounded like the foghorn at Sallishay Point on a foggy night.

Right now she was kissing up to Maisie Parsons, pretending to be sorry for her while all the time she was hoping Maisie would give her some of her gingerbread. Maisie was famous for her gingerbread. Even now, with a war on and everything on ration, somehow Maisie managed to make gingerbread that melted in your mouth, which frustrated Rita no end, particularly since Maisie steadfastly refused to divulge her secret.

They weren't talking about gingerbread right now, though. Marge's voice penetrated above the idle chatter going on among the rest of the members of the Housewives League. "You must feel so lonely without your granddaughter to help you out. What made her go back to London, then?"

"Boyfriend, I suppose." Maisie's wrinkled

face looked rather like an aging apple with her fat red cheeks and little black eyes that were almost hidden by her overlapping eyelids. "You know how the young gals are. Think they know all about love, don't they. Just wait until she's married, that's what I say. She'll soon know what's what."

Marge joined in Maisie's laughter, drowning out everyone else. "So when did she leave, then?" Marge demanded. "I thought she had a boyfriend here. Wasn't she going out with a GI?"

Maisie shrugged. "She was going out with a few of them, wasn't she. Trying to forget the one she left behind in London. I told her she was a fool to go back there, with all them bombs dropping around her, but you can't tell the young ones nothing these days. Ever since her parents were killed in that raid, she's not been the same. Heaven knows what she's up to now. I never hear from her anymore. Never bothers to write. I don't even know where she's living right now. Can't tell them anything these days. It's like she's living every day as if it was her last."

"No one's going to live very long if you don't all start listening to me!"

To Rita's immense satisfaction, at the sound of her bellow, everyone stopped talking at once and stared in her direction.

"Now," Rita said, when she was quite sure she had their undivided attention, "we are supposed to be discussing the plans for the scavenger hunt. Remember that everything we collect will be going to our brave servicemen at the front, so I want some suggestions for the scavenger hunt list. Try to keep things simple but useful." She lifted a hand as a chorus of voices answered her. "One at a time, *pulleze*. And remember now, simple but useful." She rather liked that phrase. It would make a good slogan. The Housewives League — simple but useful. Quite catching.

"Magazines," Marge announced. "When they've finished reading them they can use them to wipe their bums."

Shrieks of laughter greeted this brilliant idea.

"Quiet!" Rita thundered. She waited for the din to die down before adding, "Actually, Marjorie, that is quite a good idea. I'm sure our sailors would appreciate something to read."

"Socks!" someone else called out.

"Comics!"

"Safety pins!"

"Sticking plasters!"

"Bootlaces!"

Rita nodded after each suggestion, scribbling like mad to keep up.

"Combinations!" Maisie blurted out, apparently determined not to be outdone.

Rita narrowed her eyes amid the howls of laughter. She kept a scowl on her face until the last snicker had died down, then said icily, "This is a scavenger hunt, Maisie. The idea of a scavenger hunt is to find stuff that's just lying around that nobody wants. Or by asking people to donate things. Somehow I don't think you're going to find too many men willing to part with their underwear."

"Not clean ones, anyway," someone muttered.

Jeers of disgust threatened to drown out Rita as she attempted to keep order. Sometimes she wondered why she bothered with them. Nobody appreciated the work she did for the War Effort. Nobody. One day she'd really make them sit up and take notice. It was her dream, to become a national hero on the home front. It was all she thought about these days. The trouble was, she hadn't yet worked out how she was going to go about it. But one day she would. One fine day.

"I'm fed up." Polly slumped on the bed next to her sister, making her bounce up and down. "I hate Sundays. There's nothing to do."

Marlene tucked whatever she was reading under her pillow. "There's lots to do. You just have to look for it, that's all."

"Like what?" Polly stretched her legs out in front of her and studied her bare feet. Her toenails needed cutting. She'd love to paint them bright red, like she'd seen in the fashion magazines, but Ma would have a pink fit. Only tarts painted their toenails, she'd say.

"I dunno. Lots of things."

"All the shops are shut," Polly complained. "Even in North Horsham. You'd think they'd open up shops on a Sunday there. After all, it's a pretty big town compared to Sitting Marsh."

"Anywhere's bigger than Sitting Marsh. Anyway, even in London they don't open up the shops on Sunday." Marlene tossed her thick mane of hair back from her shoulders.

Polly scowled. Marlene was always showing off with her hair. Marlene's hair was naturally curly and a lovely shade of auburn, while Polly had to make do with dark brown hair that hung flat and straight, unless she wound it up in a knot. Of course, being a hairdresser, Marlene knew how to make the best of her hair. It wasn't fair.

Aware that her bad mood was due more to boredom than animosity toward her sister, Polly made an effort to be pleasant. "We could always go to the flicks in North Horsham, though I've seen *The Philadelphia Story* three times already, and there's a war film on at the Odeon. I don't like war films much."

"I was thinking of going down the Tudor Arms tonight." Marlene got off the bed and sat down at her dresser. "Want to go with me?"

Polly hesitated. "I don't know. I don't like going down there without Sam."

Marlene picked up a brush and started smoothing it over her hair. "You can't waste your life sitting around moping about Sam Cutter. He's a Yank, after all. One day he'll be going back to America and then you won't see him at all. Forget about him. There's plenty more fish in the ocean."

"I'll never forget him," Polly said fiercely. "Never. I'm going to marry him one day and go to America with him. So there!"

Marlene put down her brush and twisted around in her chair. "Polly, just forget it. It's over between you and Sam and the sooner you accept it the sooner you'll find someone else."

"I don't want no one else. Sam's the only one I want." Angry with her sister for not understanding, she slid off the bed. "I'll wait for him forever if I have to."

"Then you'll end up a bloody old maid." Marlene went back to brushing her hair. "Anyway, come down the pub with me tonight. It'll take your mind off him. We can ask Sadie to come, too. It's talent night, so it should be a laugh."

"All right. It's better than sitting with Ma listening to the wireless all night." Polly reached for the pillow. "What were you reading, anyhow?"

"Never you mind!" Moving so fast she startled her sister, Marlene grabbed the pillow and slapped it back on the bed. "It's just a magazine, that's all and I'm not done with it yet."

"All right, keep your bloomin' hair on." Polly sauntered over to the door. "I'm going up to the Manor House to ask Sadie about coming out tonight. She's probably finished her jobs by now."

Marlene stared at her sister's reflection in the mirror. "You're not going to chase after Sam Cutter while you're there, are you?"

31

" 'Course not!" Polly tossed her head. "I've got more pride than that, haven't I?"

"Good. I should bloomin' hope so."

"If I see him though, I'll say hello."

"Polly —"

"And invite him down the pub tonight." With a grin Polly slammed the door shut before Marlene could yell at her again.

Her sister meant well, Polly knew that. Marlene just didn't understand. That was all. Marlene's heart had been broken a lot lately, what with her American boyfriend getting killed and then that newspaper reporter from London going back to his job. Marlene was just looking out for her baby sister.

Except, Polly thought, as she ran down the stairs, it was time Marlene realized that her sister wasn't a baby anymore. She was sixteen years old. Old enough to be in love. Old enough to get married. Certainly old enough to know the right man when she met him. She and Sam were meant to be together, and that's all there was to it. And one day Sam Cutter would realize it, too. Having settled that in her mind, she hurried down the garden path to the shed to get her bike.

True to her promise, Elizabeth decided to pay a visit to the Tudor Arms later that afternoon. Opening hours weren't until seven P.M., but she knew Alfie, the barman, would be there, washing glasses and priming the pumps for the evening rush.

She preferred not to be in the pub when it was full of customers. For one thing, it was quite difficult to hold onto Alfie's attention when he was busy serving drinks, and for another, she still didn't feel comfortable visiting the Tudor Arms unescorted.

Things had changed considerably since the outbreak of the war, and with women taking up so many positions in factories, farms, and various other employment formerly held by the men, it was no longer considered bad form for a woman to be seen drinking in a public house without the benefit of a male escort.

Nevertheless, in spite of Elizabeth's streak of rebellion where old-fashioned virtues were concerned, she couldn't forget she had a position to uphold and an image to protect at all costs. Therefore, whenever possible, she observed the rules of etiquette as befitted her station.

Besides, on the rare occasion she had visited the pub during opening hours she'd been propositioned by an American airman and had to put him in his place. While secretly flattered by the attention from such a young man, she had deemed it unwise to repeat the experience.

Alfie seemed happy to see her when he answered her knock on the back door. "Your ladyship!" he exclaimed, as he held the door wide. "It's been a while since we've seen you. What brings you down here today?"

She followed him into the private lounge, bypassing the public bar, which even in these modern times was generally considered off limits to women. A strong smell of beer and cigar smoke permeated the place, almost masking the damp, musty odor that always accompanied an establishment as old as the Tudor Arms.

There were rumors that among the distinguished guests residing at the inn during its centuries of existence had been the Duke of Wellington and Edward VII, the notorious playboy king. Elizabeth could therefore vindicate any lapse in protocol by assuring herself she was, indeed, in illustrious company.

Alfie offered her the usual glass of sherry, and she graciously accepted. These days good sherry was hard to come by, and she rarely refused such a treat. After exchanging a few pleasantries, Elizabeth decided it was time to come down to business.

Seated at the long, curved bar, where gentlemen had been resting their elbows for more than four hundred years, she watched Alfie polish the glass tankards that would soon be filled with foaming ale and stout. "I trust you've been keeping well, then?" she asked, as Alfie deftly hung a tankard on a hook above his head. "I've been hearing about a mysterious illness going around. I hope it hasn't affected any of your customers?"

Alfie went on polishing the next glass, conveniently pretending he didn't know she was fishing for information. "Not as far as I know, m'm. Nasty business that, what with them dying and all."

"Indeed." Elizabeth sipped delicately at her sherry. "How tragic for their families to lose them that way."

Alfie glanced over at the door as if expecting someone to come through it any minute. Then he leaned across the counter and in a low voice muttered, "That's if they did die from an illness. The Yanks could just be saying that to cover up the real reason. If you ask me, it's them three musketeers getting up to their tricks again. Only this time they might have gone a bit too far."

Elizabeth stared at him in astonishment. "Three musketeers? I thought they died centuries ago. Whatever are you talking about?"

"Not what." Alfie put a finger alongside his nose. "Who. And they're very much alive. That's what people call them — the three musketeers. Come down from London now and again. Don't know if there's really three of 'em, or if there's more, but they're a nasty bit of work. Got it in for the Yanks, they have, and spend their time doing their best to antagonize 'em. Up until now it's been pretty harmless, though they've been known to do some damage to their Jeeps in the past."

"You think these people are poisoning the Americans?"

It was Alfie's turn to look startled. "Who said anything about poison?"

Inwardly cursing her runaway tongue, Elizabeth said carelessly, "Oh, it was just a rumor I heard. Someone said the men who died might have had food poisoning."

"Well, they didn't get it in here. I eat here all the time and I'd have been sick too if our food was bad." He nodded at a jar of pickled eggs on the counter. "That's what most of 'em eat down here, that and crisps. Sometimes we have sausage rolls, but what with the rationing and all, we don't get them very often anymore."

"But what about these people you call musketeers? Do they ever come in here?"

"Nah." Alfie rubbed his cloth vigorously against the side of a gleaming tankard. "No one has seen them. Don't even know what they look like. They leave their mark behind, though, wherever they go. Three Ms, all linked together. That's how they got the name of the three musketeers."

A harsh male voice spoke from behind Elizabeth, startling her. "If you ask me, they are doing us all a big favor."

Alfie nodded at the newcomer, who had entered silently through the main door. "Evening, Dick." He tipped his head at Elizabeth. "This is Lady Elizabeth, from the Manor House on the hill. Dick Adelaide, your ladyship. He bought the dairy farm out on the coast road a few months ago."

"Oh, yes," Elizabeth murmured. "I heard it had been sold. I've been meaning to come down and visit your wife."

The bearded man touched the brim of his cap. "Your ladyship. Pleasure to meet you, m'm."

"Likewise, I'm sure."

Elizabeth watched as the burly farmer handed over a large basket that appeared to be filled with slabs of butter and cheese as well as a dozen or so eggs. His clothes reeked of tobacco smoke, and something else she didn't want to think about.

"There you go, mate!" he said, as Alfie took the basket from him. "That should do you for a while."

Alfie disappeared for a moment behind the counter, then reappeared holding two bottles of Scotch. "Better put these under your coat," he said, handing them to Dick. "We don't want to start a rumble."

The farmer gave Elizabeth a sheepish smile. "Seems there's better things to fight about than a couple of bottles of Scotch, don't it?"

"Indeed." Elizabeth narrowed her eyes. "What did you mean just now, about people doing everyone a favor?"

Alfie loudly cleared his throat, but Dick Adelaide seemed oblivious to the apparent warning. "Well, I think the sooner we get rid of them blasted Americans, the better," he said gruffly. "I don't care how they do it. If it takes a gang of hooligans to get them out of town, then so good."

"So you think we can win this war without them, then," Elizabeth said pleasantly.

A look of uncertainty crossed the farmer's face. "I don't mean no disrespect, m'm, but in my mind this place would be a lot better off without the GIs chasing after every bit of skirt they set eyes on. They're troublemakers, the lot of them. I wish they'd go back where they belong."

"Troublemakers?" Elizabeth was doing her best to hold her temper, but she could feel her cheeks growing warm and her fingers clenching in her lap. "These men, who risk losing their lives every day to help us fight this dreadful war, are nothing but troublemakers? I wonder how they'd feel if they heard you speak of them that way. How motivated do you think they'd be, given how you feel, to go through the gates of hell to save your skin?"

"Begging your pardon, your ladyship, I know the risks the lads are taking, but that doesn't give them the right to ruin innocent young lives. Now, if you'll excuse me, I have to get back to my work." He nodded at Alfie, who looked as if he were about to choke. "Thanks, mate. See you tomorrow." He gave Elizabeth a frosty look. "Your ladyship."

"Good day," Elizabeth said stiffly. She waited until the door had swung behind the belligerent farmer, then let out her breath in an explosion of wrath. "Well I never! What an abominable man. It's that kind of thinking that causes all the trouble in Sitting Marsh. I'd like to beat some sense into that dense brain of his."

38

Alfie tucked the basket under the counter, then said a little awkwardly, "Don't let him get you upset, your ladyship. He's not a bad chap, really. It's his daughter what got him like that. I heard as how some GI got her . . ." he paused, cleared his throat, then mumbled, "gave her a bun in the oven, so to speak. She went to some quack in North Horsham. He botched the job and she died. Annie, that's Dick's wife, hasn't been the same since. Dick don't have a good word for the Americans now."

Having heard all she wanted to for the time being, Elizabeth slipped off her stool. "Well, while the poor man has my deepest sympathy for the loss of his daughter, I do wish he would remember that it takes two to tango."

Alfie's lips twitched. "Yes, m'm."

"You will let me know if anyone else should fall ill, won't you, Alfie?"

"That I will, m'm."

She paused at the door, looking back at him. "Oh, and if you should learn anything more about these musketeer people, I'd be obliged if you'd give me a ring. I'd like to know who it is harassing our American military so that I can take steps to put a stop to it. It's bad enough that we have this kind of trouble in the village, but when the source comes from as far away as London, that is a matter of grave concern."

"I quite agree, m'm." Alfie lifted his hand. "If I find out anything at all, you'll be the first to know."

"Thank you, Alfie." She stepped out into the bright rays of the setting sun, a deep feeling of unease unsettling her. It was one thing to deal with the villagers, with whom she was familiar and understood their ways, but Alfie's mention of a gang of hooligans from London was a different matter altogether.

George and Sid did what they could, but they were reluctant constables at best, having been dragged out of retirement to replace the younger men called up for the military. As for the local inspector, he had been absent so long Elizabeth had more or less forgotten what he looked like. He would be no match for a determined band of vigilantes from London. It would be up to her to take care of the matter, and she wasn't sure if she was up to the task.

Then there was the matter of Dick Adelaide. It had occurred to her that he had a very strong reason for hating the Americans. Enough to kill? It was a sobering thought.

It wasn't often she felt vulnerable, but right then, she would have given the world to see Earl's reassuring figure striding toward her.

The thought scared her. She was beginning to depend on him. That wouldn't do at all. The problem was, she couldn't seem to help it. And that could only mean trouble for her, and eventually, maybe for Earl, too.

Chapter 3

When Polly arrived at the Manor House, Sadie had finished her chores and was in her room. The moment Sadie opened the door to Polly's knock, she grabbed the younger girl's arm and dragged her inside.

"What's the matter with you?" Polly demanded, staring at the housemaid with wide eyes.

Sadie's face was flushed with excitement. "You'll never guess who I saw," she said, as Polly flopped down on the narrow bed. "Right in front of my bloody eyes, he was. I couldn't believe it."

"Cary Grant," Polly said promptly.

Sadie dropped onto the only chair in the room. "Don't be daft. What would Cary Grant be doing in Sitting Marsh?"

"Making a film, that's what." Polly wriggled her bare toes, enjoying the freedom of her new sandals. They had platform soles, with just two thin straps holding them on her feet. They weren't too comfortable, and made pedaling her bicycle a little dodgy, but she loved the look of them. She'd used up all her clothing coupons and waited two months for weather warm enough to wear them. It had been worth it. It made her feel like Betty Grable in *Moon Over Miami*.

"Making a film? In this dump? Not bloody likely, is it." Sadie peered in the mirror. "Do you think my hair looks better tied back in bunches or around my face?"

Polly stared at the other girl's reflection in the mirror. Sadie's hair was a shiny dark brown and too short to be worn in bunches. They stuck out from the sides of her head, and from the back she looked like the Pekingese Polly's Aunt Mathilda used to have.

"Around your face," she told Sadie. "Makes you look more glamorous. Who did you see then?"

"Guess!" Sadie spun around and hugged herself. "You'll never get it in a million years."

"Well, tell me if he's a film star."

"Nah, better than that."

"King George, then."

Sadie grinned. "You're getting warmer."

Polly glared at her in frustration. "Why don't you just tell me."

"All right." Sadie pulled in a deep breath. "I saw Winston Churchill. Right here on the coast road."

Polly stared for a moment longer, then broke into peals of laughter. "Winnie? Here in Sitting Marsh? Did he have his bulldog with him?"

"No, he didn't," Sadie said stiffly. "He was walking along the cliffs, staring down at the beach."

"All by himself?" Polly giggled again. "What did you do? Ask him if he was lost?"

"I said good morning. I was on my bicycle. Violet sent me out to the Millers' farm to get some rhubarb, and I was on my way back when I seen him."

Polly shook her head. "Sadie, what would Winston Churchill be doing here when he's supposed to be in London fighting the war? It must have been someone what looked like him."

"It was him, I tell you. I know it sounds strange, but I swear it was him."

"Well, don't swear too hard or Violet will be after you." Polly got off the bed. "I came here to ask if you wanted to go down the pub with Marlene and me tonight."

"All right. Don't believe it. But I know what I saw." Sadie peered in the mirror again. "What time are you going to the pub tonight, then?"

"I don't know. About half past seven, I suppose. It only takes a few minutes to get there on our bicycles."

Sadie got up from her chair. "You seen Sam lately?"

"Not lately, no."

"Is he going to be down the Arms?"

Polly shrugged. "Don't think so. He hasn't been there since he smashed up his face in that accident. He don't like going out with all them scars on his face."

"Silly bugger. He's the only one what worries about his face. No one else cares about it."

43

Polly hurried to the door. The subject of Sam was still painful and she didn't like talking about it. "See you tonight, then." She started to close the door then poked her head around it. "You can bring Winnie if you like." She shut the door just before the box of face powder that Sadie threw could hit her in the face.

Sadie's room was on the lowest floor of the mansion, just down the hall from the kitchen. It was always quiet on a Sunday. It was Polly's day off so she wasn't there much on Sundays anymore. Not like when she used to be the housemaid.

Polly used to like being in the Manor House on Sundays. Martin always rested in his room in the afternoons, and Violet, having cooked a large meal midday, usually took a nap in her quarters.

Right now most of the American airmen billeted in the east wing were either at the base or spending the day in North Horsham. By that evening, though, a lot of them would be back for the talent night at the Tudor Arms. It was closer to the base, and they wouldn't have so far to drive. Which was just as well if they'd had too much to drink. Most of them had trouble remembering to drive on the left side of the road, even when they were sober.

Polly and her sister had come close to being run over many times on the way back from the pub. In fact, that's how she'd met Sam. He'd put them both in the ditch while driving on the wrong side of the road.

Polly smiled at the memory, but her smile soon faded. Things had been really good between them until Sam had found out how old she was. She'd lied about her age because she was afraid he'd think she was too young. Then, when he found out the truth, he was so flaming angry he'd driven around a bend too fast and overturned the Jeep. He hadn't wanted anything to do with her ever since.

Polly climbed the huge curving staircase to the second floor, her heart heavy with the pain of it all. He'd come to Sunday tea once, but she'd hardly seen him since then. Sadie and Marlene thought he was staying away from her because of his scars. Polly wanted very badly to believe that, but a niggling worry deep inside her whispered that Sam didn't want her anymore because she was too young for him. Sam was going to be twenty-five this year. It might as well have been forty-five, the way he felt about it.

Polly reached the top of the stairs and paused, struck by the sudden icy chill that seemed to close in around her. The sun was still high in the sky, and would be for several hours, thanks to double summertime. Even so, the great hall was thick with shadows, most of the sunlight obscured by heavy velvet curtains and the thick dust on the towering windows.

In her thin sleeveless blouse, Polly shivered.

Ahead of her the great hall stretched the length of the manor, its walls peppered with solemn portraits of former earls of Wellsborough and their ladies.

About midway down, a massive suit of armor kept guard over the silent walls. It was just beyond there that Polly thought she saw the shadow of a man, moving stealthily along the right wall.

Goosebumps raised themselves all the way down her arms. Rumors that the Manor House was haunted had been passed around the village ever since Polly could remember. No one had ever actually seen a ghost. Except Martin, of course, and everyone knew that Martin had a screw loose.

But now Polly wasn't so sure. Someone was moving down there, and she could see right through him. She opened her mouth to scream, but no sound came out. Frozen in one spot, she could only stare as the shadowy figure seemed to merge with the curtains, then disappear.

In that moment another movement from the end of the hall caught her eye. Her breath came out in a rush of relief as she realized the man heading toward her was solid flesh and bone, then she lost her breath again when she saw it was Sam.

He barely limped now, and the angry red patches of scars had faded to a light pink. Every day he was beginning to look more and more like the old Sam. Her heart contracted with

46

pain. It was too bad he didn't act like the old Sam. How she missed being with him.

He greeted her with a raised hand as he drew close. "Hi there. What are you up to?"

He paused in front of her, and she ached to rush up to him and fling her arms around him and never let go. "Hello, Sam. You'll never guess what I just saw."

His eyes were wary as he studied her face. "Okay, I give up. What did you just see?"

"A blinking ghost, that's what." She pointed at the window further down the hall. "Right there. He walked right into them curtains and disappeared."

Sam shook his head. "You sound like that old clown, Martin. I thought he was the one seeing ghosts."

Unsure herself now of what she really did see, Polly let it drop. "It's nice to see you, Sam. I was hoping I'd bump into you. I wanted to ask you something."

Her stomach seemed to drop as the dreaded remote look crossed his face. "Like what?"

"Well, *The Philadelphia Story* is on at the cinema in North Horsham and I was wondering if you'd like to go with me to see it?"

"Sorry, I've already seen it."

"Oh." Her disappointment was crushing, but she struggled to seem unaffected by the brush off. "Well, then, how about the war movie that's on at the Odeon? I can't remember what it's called, but —"

"I've seen that, too." Sam looked at his watch. "Look, I'm sorry Polly, but I gotta run. I'll catch up with you later, all right?"

Miserably, she watched him stride away from her. At the last minute, just before he reached the stairs, she called out after him. "I'm going down the Tudor Arms tonight with Marlene. Are you going to be there?"

"Sorry. Can't make it." His answer floated back to her, and then he was gone.

She felt like crying, but bit back the tears. So it was going to take some time, that's all. Sooner or later she'd wear him down, and then things would get back to normal between them. She just had to keep working at it, and not give up. Ever.

Instead of returning to the Manor House, Elizabeth decided to pay a call on the new tenants of the dairy farm. After all, she assured herself, it was only common courtesy to welcome them to Sitting Marsh, even if it was a trifle belated.

A flock of crows erupted from the branches of a gnarled oak tree, cawing their displeasure as her motorbike shattered the peaceful countryside with its harsh roar. Guiltily Elizabeth shut off the engine. The gruesome noise was the only drawback to her chosen method of transportation.

She loved the freedom of riding head on into the salty wind fresh from the ocean, and the sense of being somehow adrift from the bounds of earth. At times it made her feel as if she were flying, and she loved the idea that in an odd way, she was experiencing similar sensations as Earl might feel in his airplane. As if they shared something very special.

Laughing at her foolish notions, she climbed off her noisy steed and straightened her skirt. It was rather a nuisance to be hampered by skirts when she rode the motorcycle. She'd have much preferred wearing those baggy trousers that the Land Army girls wore. So much more accommodating, even if they were ghastly unattractive. But a lady of the manor couldn't be caught dead in such atrocious attire.

Protocol demanded that she be dressed properly in public at all times, which meant a frock and a beastly hat, which had to be heavily anchored with pins and ribbons and did dreadful things to her hair. More often than not the hat would become dislodged and flap around in a most annoying manner.

She'd lost more than a few hats completely when they had sailed from her head and disappeared over the cliffs. Consequently she learned to choose hats with a short brim. Or no brim at all. Which left her face exposed to the elements and would no doubt age her before her time.

Pondering on the miseries of being too poor to buy an automobile, Elizabeth trudged up a stony path to a delightful porch wreathed in fragrant clematis. The house was built of white stone, and the thatched roof overhung almost to the top of the latticed windows.

Elizabeth lifted the heavy black iron knocker and let it fall. It was in the shape of a horse's head, and she was still studying it when the door creaked open.

The woman who stood in the doorway almost filled the entire space with her massive hips and bosom. Her dark hair was coiled tightly around her head, and sad blue eyes peered out from under puffy lids. She didn't speak, but waited with a sort of resigned, empty look on her face that struck Elizabeth as being completely without interest or hope.

"How do you do?" Elizabeth said briskly, offering her gloved hand. "I'm Lady Elizabeth Hartleigh Compton from the Manor House. I do apologize for not visiting before this, but things have been rather hectic lately. The war, you know. Keeps one very busy."

"It does indeed," the woman said. Her voice, like her face, was lifeless. "I'm pleased to meet you, your ladyship. I'm Annie Adelaide. Won't you come in?" She stood back to allow Elizabeth to enter.

Squeezing past the decidedly buxom woman, Elizabeth entered the parlor, which was tastefully furnished and impeccably clean. Sadie should see what a house could look like when the work was done properly, Elizabeth thought darkly.

"What a pleasant room," she remarked, drawing her gloves from her hands.

Annie Adelaide looked around the room as if

seeing it for the first time. "Thank you. Won't you sit down? Can I offer you some tea? Or would you prefer a glass of sherry?"

"Oh, sherry, please," Elizabeth said quickly. Things were beginning to look up, she thought, as she settled herself in a comfy armchair that had seen better days.

Annie left the room, and Elizabeth studied her surroundings with interest. Vases of flowers stood on pedestals and tables in every corner. In one corner in particular, a framed photograph of a young girl was flanked by candles, and tiny bunches of forget-me-nots.

Elizabeth guessed this was the daughter and got up to take a closer look. Such a beautiful child, with wide, trusting brown eyes and a gentle mouth. What a tragedy. No wonder her father had such an unfortunate attitude.

"That was my youngest, Barbara," a soft voice said behind her. "She died two months ago."

Elizabeth put down the mother-of-pearl frame and returned to her chair. "I'm so very sorry. You must find it very difficult to talk about her."

"It is, m'm. But then again, sometimes it helps." Annie laid the tray she carried on a small table. On it were two glasses of sherry, a plate filled with cream crackers and a surprising selection of cheeses. She handed one of the glasses to Elizabeth, then filled a tea plate with crackers and slices of cheese and balanced it on the arm of Elizabeth's chair.

Elizabeth glanced at the plate with apprehension. There was enough on there to kill her appetite for the next two days, yet it would be churlish not to eat it all.

She watched Annie pile her own plate up with food. No wonder the woman was so large. She waited until Annie had settled herself into an armchair, then said gently, "Do you feel like talking about her now? You said her name was Barbara?"

Annie stuffed a large cracker loaded with cheese in her mouth and chewed it down before answering. "Yes, m'm. She were only sixteen. She got in the family way, by one of them GIs at the base. He wanted her to get rid of it, so she took the money and went to North Horsham to find a doctor who'd do it for her. I don't know where she found the one who did it, but he weren't no doctor, I can tell you that. He cut her up so bad she couldn't stop the bleeding. Dick found her in the bathroom." For a brief moment she paused, then added quietly, "It was too late to help her by then. My baby died on the way to the hospital."

"How utterly awful for you. I'm so sorry. Your husband must have been devastated."

Although she didn't feel at all like eating, Elizabeth reached for a cracker and the smallest slice of cheese she could find. After nibbling for a moment or two, she murmured, "I hope that man is in prison for what he did."

Annie stuffed more food in her mouth. When

she could finally speak she muttered, "We never found out who he was. Nor the Yank who got Barbara into trouble. They got away with murder, the two of them."

"And the police couldn't help?"

"What police?" Annie uttered a mirthless laugh. "Those fools in the village did nothing. My husband went to the base and they said they couldn't help him. No one cared that my beautiful daughter bled to death." Her voice finally broke, giving Elizabeth some relief. Up until then she was afraid the poor woman had lost touch with her feelings.

"There, there," she murmured, "I can understand how you feel. Did Barbara not talk about her boyfriend?"

"Oh, she talked about him. Said his name was Buddy. That weren't his real name, though. The man at the base told Dick that a lot of the GIs have that nickname. Barbara never told us his last name."

"And you never saw him?"

Annie stuffed more food in her mouth, chewed with the determination of a cow with a mouthful of cud, then said bitterly, "Once. I spotted her with him in the town. Went by me in one of them Jeeps, they did. I wish I'd been able to stop them, I might have been able to say something, do something to save her, but they went by so fast. She didn't even see me. Not that she would have listened, anyway. She might have been my youngest, but she had a mind of her own, she did. Not like her brothers and sister."

"Oh, so you do have other children," Elizabeth said, in hopes of lightening the conversation. "That must be of some comfort to you."

"It would be if they were here." Once more Annie forced food down her throat, then washed it down with a gulp of sherry that must have burned her throat. "The boys are away in the navy," she added, when she'd digested the load. "Jennifer, my eldest, she's a nurse in a London hospital."

"Oh, I'm sorry. You must miss them all." Elizabeth sipped her sherry, then introduced the question uppermost in her mind. "Did your husband ever see Barbara's boyfriend?"

"No, m'm. Never. He'd have killed him if he'd ever set eyes on him."

Elizabeth put her glass down so quickly she spilled some of the sherry. "Was this young man wearing a hat when you saw him, by any chance?"

Annie frowned. "I think so, m'm. Can't say as I remember, to tell the truth."

"Ah, then you didn't notice the color of his hair."

"His hair? No. I really didn't get a good look at him. I s'pose I was too busy looking at Barbara to pay him much attention."

"I would imagine so." Elizabeth looked at her plate, wondering how she was going to finish all the cheese on it.

As if reading her mind, Annie said quickly, "Please don't feel you have to eat all that, m'm. I know I sometimes go overboard when I give someone food. I eat too much myself. Can't seem to stop eating these days. All I want to do is eat, as if I have to have something in my mouth to keep going, if you know what I mean."

"Yes, I quite understand." With relief Elizabeth got up and put her plate and glass down on the table. "Sometimes it helps to have something else to concentrate on."

"Yes, mum." Annie heaved herself out of her chair. "It's just as well everything's rationed, or I'd be twice as huge."

Her heart aching for the woman, Elizabeth held out her hand. "I'm truly sorry to hear about your daughter. I hope that in time you can think of her without so much pain."

"The only way I'm going to be free of pain, m'm," Annie said, in a voice so quiet Elizabeth could hardly hear her, "is to see that butchering so-called doctor rotting in prison where he can't hurt no more young girls like my Barbara."

"Well, perhaps I can do something about that," Elizabeth said impulsively. "I can't promise of course, but I'll see what I can do."

"Thank you, m'm." A vestige of a smile flickered across Annie's face. "That would make me and Dick feel easier in our minds. There's such a lot of this kind of thing going on, but somehow you never think it'll happen to someone right in your own family."

Elizabeth returned to her motorcycle, the unfortunate woman's words repeating in her mind. Somehow she would track down the despicable monster who had done this dreadful thing.

Somehow you never think it'll happen to someone right in your own family. She could say the same about her own situation, Elizabeth reflected with a stab of guilt. She would never have imagined herself involved with a married man. In fact, until it had happened to her, she had deemed such women as heartless harlots without a decent bone in their bodies.

She'd read so many stories about women caught up in wartime romance who invariably ended up with a broken heart. It would seem that she was doomed not to find happiness with a man. She could have accepted that if it weren't for the fact that she was desperately in love with Major Earl Monroe, and there wasn't a blessed thing she could do about it.

Chapter 4

Later that evening Elizabeth was delighted when Violet came to tell her that Earl wanted to speak to her. Seated in her favorite refuge, the conservatory, she waited eagerly for the light tap on the door that would announce his arrival.

When it came, she felt a ridiculous fluttering in her stomach, and her voice sounded a trifle breathless when she called out for him to enter.

The dogs, who had been lying contentedly at her feet, scrambled up and greeted him with tails furiously wagging. He squatted on his haunches to ruffle their ears, and his eyes crinkled at the edges when he looked at her. "I figured you'd be here in your little hideaway."

She returned his smile without looking directly at him, fearful of giving away her intense pleasure at the sight of him. "I think the dogs would prefer to be out there chasing each other on the lawn. I love this time of year. The light evenings mean I can sit and look at the gardens, instead of staring at that ugly blackout curtain. By the time we have to draw them, it's almost time for bed."

He rose to his feet and stood with his back to her, his gaze on the rolling lawns. The windows in front of him stretched from floor to ceiling, giving the impression that the entire wall was made of glass. "This is the most peaceful room I've ever been in."

Something in his voice alerted her. "What is it, Earl? Is something wrong?"

He stood for a moment longer, then came back to her side and lowered himself onto the wicker rocker. The sight of him gently rocking back and forth was so dear and familiar to her. She looked upon the chair as "his chair," and knew that once he returned to America, as one day he must, she would never allow anyone else to sit on it. She would move it to her office and keep it enshrined there.

"I guess I'm just upset about the death of these guys. It's such a damn waste." He flicked a glance at her. "Sorry, Elizabeth."

"I've told you before," she said mildly, "you don't have to apologize. Using swear words and cursing is a national pastime in this country nowadays. I even indulge in it myself now and again."

He grinned at her. "Isn't that considered a mortal sin for a lady of the manor?"

She wrinkled her nose at him. "I'm guilty of quite a few indiscretions that might be considered a mortal sin for one in my position. So far I've managed to prevail in spite of them. Being here alone with you, for instance."

She had no idea where those last words had come from and instantly wished them back.

Earl gave her one of those looks that made her insides quiver. "Well, I guess you're safe enough. There's no chance of hanky-panky with Violet hovering around outside like an avenging angel."

Shaken by the thought of indulging in anything remotely resembling hanky-panky with him, she said faintly, "Violet is hovering outside?"

He shrugged, his gaze still intent on her face. "Well, I have to go through her every time I want to see you, which kind of cuts down on any chance of anything private or . . . intimate."

She seemed to have a great deal of trouble drawing breath, which resulted in her voice emitting a squeak. *"Intimate?"*

"Are you really that scared of me?"

She searched his face, expecting to see teasing in his eyes. Instead she saw he was serious, even a little offended. Impulsively she leaned forward and covered his warm hand with her own. "Oh, Earl I have never been scared of you. I trust you implicitly. You have never been anything but a perfect gentleman."

"Yeah, I know."

Something about the way he said it sent a thrill throughout her body. She'd heard regret in his voice and . . . dare she even think it? Longing. An echo of her own hopeless yearning for something they could never have.

Suddenly and quite acutely aware of her fingers resting on his thigh, she quickly withdrew her hand. "I'm glad you stopped by," she said, in a voice that was decidedly shaky. "I wanted to talk to you about something I heard today."

Stubbornly ignoring the disappointment in his eyes, she recounted everything she'd heard about Dick and Annie Adelaide. "It did occur to me," she said, when she'd finished repeating her conversation with Annie, "that since Mr. Adelaide despises Americans so much, he has a motive for at least one of the recent deaths. I wonder if any of those poor young men were called Buddy?"

Earl had sat rocking while listening to her story, and now he halted the gentle swaying of the chair. "Well, that's one of the reasons I came to see you. The test results came back from the lab."

Elizabeth's interest sharpened at once. "Really? What did they say?"

Earl sighed and clasped his hands around a knee. "According to the medics, the guys did die of poisoning. But it looks as if the poison came from a plant. They were probably eating wild berries. Some of those babies are deadly poisonous."

Elizabeth looked at him curiously. "Is that what they really think? That it's accidental poisoning?"

Earl shrugged. "That's what they're saying right now."

"And how do they explain the phenomena of all the victims having red hair?"

"Coincidence?"

"You surely don't believe that."

"No, I don't." He lifted his hands and let them drop. "That's the official verdict right now, which means there'll be no investigation. I think they're afraid of opening a can of worms. They have no proof it was deliberate, and until they do, they can't do much about it. Officially, I have to abide by that."

"And unofficially?"

He looked sheepish. "I was kind of hoping you'd look into it."

She smiled.

"Just as long as there's no danger involved," he added hurriedly.

"Of course."

"What about this dairy farmer? Do you really think he might have something to do with it?"

"I don't know." She frowned. "He certainly had a strong enough motive to hate at least one American airman. But why kill the others? Simply because they reminded him of his daughter's boyfriend? I find that hard to believe. Did your medics mention what kind of berries?"

Earl shook his head. "The report named the poisons. Mezerin, I think. Something like that. And something that sounded like a girl's name. Began with a D. Diana . . . no, Doris . . . wait a minute . . ."

While he thought about it she got to her feet. "I'll be back in a minute," she said. "I believe I have a book on poisonous plants in the library.

I'll take a look. Would you care for some sherry or would you rather have a short?"

He raised his eyebrows. "Short?"

"You know, a short drink. Like Scotch, or gin."

"Oh!" His frown cleared. "Scotch sounds good."

"Right. I'll have Violet fetch it for you." She left him alone and headed for the kitchen. After giving Violet instructions to take both Scotch and sherry to the conservatory, she ran up the stairs to the library.

It took her longer than she intended to find the book, and she hurried back to the conservatory, half afraid Earl had given up on her and left.

When she pushed open the door, however, he was still there in the rocker, head back, drink in hand, his eyes closed. He looked so peaceful and rested she hated to disturb him, but as she crept across the floor to the white wicker couch he opened his eyes.

"Hope you don't mind me starting without you," he said, raising the crystal glass.

"Of course not." She saw that he'd poured her a glass of sherry, and smiled her thanks. "There's nothing like a glass of good sherry to relax one at the end of the day." She sank onto the couch and opened up the book. "Now, you say it began with D. Have you thought of it, yet?"

"Nope. It's not a common name, I know that."

Elizabeth began reading down the index.

"Oh, my, there's so many poisonous plants. I had no idea. Ah, here we are. There's only one that begins with a D. Good Lord. Daphne?"

"That's it!" Earl sat up so fast his Scotch slurped around in the glass. "I knew it was a girl's name."

"All parts are poisonous," Elizabeth read out loud. "The fruit is especially deadly. The poisons are daphnetoxin and mezerein. Heating or cooking doesn't kill toxicity. Symptoms include severe burning of mouth and throat, acute enteritis, kidney damage, convulsions, coma, ending in death." She snapped the book closed. "Those poor souls. How they must have suffered. I had no idea the plant was so toxic."

"Do you know what it looks like?"

"Why, yes." She waved a hand at the windows. "We probably have some right here in the gardens. I'm not an expert on gardening, but I believe it's a very popular ornamental plant and grows well in our climate."

Earl shook his head. "I can't believe those guys would be stupid enough to eat berries without knowing what they were."

"Who knows what young men do when they've had too much to drink." Elizabeth laid the book down beside her. "Then again, they might not have known they were eating them. Someone could easily crush up the berries and drop them into a glass of stout. You did say that each of the men who died spent his last night at the Tudor Arms, didn't you?"

"I did." Earl ran a hand through his springy hair. "I can't believe that someone out there hates us enough to do something that gruesome."

"Which brings us back to Dick Adelaide." Elizabeth reached for her sherry. "I think I'll take a ride past the dairy farm again tomorrow. Just to see if there's any daphne growing in the garden."

"You will be careful, Elizabeth?"

She felt warmed by his concern. "Aren't I always?"

His shout of laughter took her by surprise. "How many times have I had to barge in and rescue you?"

"Ah, I do that on purpose. Just so you can feel chivalrous."

Again his grin lightened her heart. "You like the idea of a white knight charging to the rescue on his horse?"

"I like the idea of you charging to the rescue." Again she had spoken impulsively, and quickly added, "You are far more reliable than our local constabulary."

He sighed, and put down his glass. "Trust the United States Army Air Force to get the job done, right?" He glanced at his watch. "It's time I got going. Thanks for the Scotch."

"No need to thank me. You brought us two bottles last week from the base." She watched him rise to his feet, already feeling the pain of loss. It could be days before she saw him again.

How she hated this beastly war. Then again, without it, she would never have had these precious moments with him.

"Then I thank you for the very pleasant company. Just promise me you won't do anything rash."

He pulled on his cap, and her heart turned over. How handsome he looked in his uniform. "I promise." She jumped up, disturbing the dogs once more. "I'll simply ask a few questions, and I'll drop in on the constables, just in case they happen to have some useful information. George can be very tight-lipped at times, but Sid, bless his heart, can't keep a still tongue in his head."

Earl seemed unconvinced. "I don't like asking you to get involved in this, but if someone had it in for these guys and deliberately poisoned them, I want to know. It's hard enough to lose them in battle, but to lose them this way breaks my heart. I hate to see the whole thing brushed under the mat like this but my hands are tied."

Against her better judgement she moved closer to him and laid her hand on his arm. "Don't worry, Earl. I'll do everything in my power to ferret out what really happened to those men."

"I know you will." He looked down at her hand resting on his arm, then reached for it. Slowly he raised it and pressed his lips to her fingers. "I don't know what I'd do without you now. You make it all bearable."

Unexpected tears stung her eyes. "I'm glad." She pulled her hand from his grasp. "Don't stay away so long next time."

"I'll try not to." He looked down at her for a long moment, until she thought she would suffocate from holding her breath. Then, with a muttered "Good night," he twisted away from her and disappeared through the door.

It wasn't until an hour or so later that she realized she hadn't told him about the three musketeers Alfie had talked about. Ah well, it would give her a good excuse to talk to Earl again soon. Right now she was ready to grasp every opportunity she could get.

"I swear this place gets more bloomin' crowded every time we come down here." Sadie lifted a glass tankard of foaming beer and gulped several mouthfuls of it before putting it back down.

Seated across from her, Polly looked on in amazement. She'd never liked the taste of beer, and couldn't understand how Sadie managed to drink so much of it. She'd be peeing all night long if she drank half that much.

"It's getting noisier, too." Sadie twisted her head to scan the room. "Can't see anything interesting yet, can you, Marl?"

Marlene shrugged. "Not much, no."

Sadie narrowed her eyes. "That bloke over there looks a bit of all right. Got a nice bum, he has. Wouldn't mind putting my hands on that."

Marlene looked shocked, while Polly giggled. "Gawd, if Ma heard us talking like that she'd take the poker to us," she said. "Anyway, I thought you was bringing Winnie down here with you tonight."

Marlene stared at her sister. "Who's Winnie?"

"Winston Churchill hisself, that's who." Polly pointed a finger at Sadie. "Ask her how she met him."

Marlene turned her astonished gaze on Sadie. "You met Winston Churchill?"

"I didn't say as how I met him," Sadie said, glaring at Polly. "I said as how I *seen* him. Up on the cliffs. I said good morning to him, but he didn't answer me. Just sort of nodded, you know the way he does, then went on walking with his head down."

"Can't see as how you did that," Polly said scornfully, "when he spoke on the wireless last night. He'd have to fly down here to get here that fast."

"Well, maybe he did," Sadie said smugly. "After all, if anyone can get a ride on a plane it would be our Winnie, right?"

"Well, I don't believe you saw him, so there."

Marlene shook her head. "It couldn't have been him, Sadie. What would he be doing in Sitting Marsh?"

Sadie raised her shoulders and let them drop. "How the bloody hell do I know? Watching for an invasion, more than likely. He's always talking about one, ain't he?"

Marlene's mouth tugged into a smile, then she exploded into a fit of giggles. "Maybe he just wanted a paddle in the sea."

"He'd have to pick his way through the land mines," Polly said, joining in the laughter.

Sadie's cheeks turned pink. "I don't care what no one says, I saw him and that's that. Anyhow, I'd rather have my hands on that Yank over there than Winnie anytime."

Polly followed Sadie's gaze to where a group of GIs lounged against the bar. "Which one is he, anyway?"

"That one on the right." Sadie jerked her head in that direction. "The tall one with the blond hair."

Polly looked. "He's all right, but he's nothing next to my Sam." The ache was back in her stomach. "I wish he was down here. I miss him so much."

Marlene snorted. "What you need is another boyfriend."

Polly shook her head. "Don't want no one but Sam."

"Your sister's right," Sadie said, her gaze still directed at the bar. "The best medicine for a broken heart is a new bloke."

"If I can't have Sam I don't want no one." Polly picked up her gin and orange and threw most of it down her throat. Choking, she had to wait until she got her breath back before adding hoarsely, "Even if I have to be an old maid for the rest of me life."

Sadie gave her a pitying look. "You're only sixteen. You got lots of time to find the right bloke for you. These Yanks are all right to have some fun with, but none of them wants to get bleeding married. They'll be back in America at the end of the war."

"And that's where I'm going. Back with Sam." Polly stared defiantly at Sadie. "So there."

Sadie's scornful laugh exploded across the table. "Don't be bleeding daft. Whatcha want to go to America for? You could get your head shot off. They all got guns there. Everyone has 'em."

"No they don't." Polly fought back tears. "They have nice houses and swimming pools and mountains and everything."

Sadie rolled her eyes. "I can tell you've been watching too many of them American films. Real life ain't like that, Polly, and you'd better know what you're getting into if you go to America."

"She's not going to America," Marlene said firmly. "Ma would never let her go. She's too young."

"Well, I wouldn't want to go. Would you?"

Marlene smiled. "Not me. I got bigger plans than that."

Polly glared at Marlene. "What's that supposed to mean?"

"Never you mind." Marlene turned to Sadie. "Are you going to sing in the talent show tonight?"

69

Sadie shrugged. "Don't know. I haven't had enough beer yet."

Polly sat back in her chair, hoping the pain under her ribs would go away. Marlene never kept secrets from her until lately. Something was up with her big sister, and Polly wanted very badly to know what was going on. It wasn't like Marlene to shut her out. They'd shared everything together, but lately Marlene seemed to be shutting herself away in a world of her own. She didn't even understand about her wanting to go to America.

Perhaps she should have another gin. Though even that didn't help when she thought about Sam going to America without her.

Throughout the rest of the evening she sat wishing she was somewhere else. Preferably with Sam, of course. Anywhere, as long as it was with Sam.

Sadie was persuaded to get up on the microphone, where she bellowed out a rowdy version of "My Old Man's a Dustman," then had everyone up to do "Knees up Mother Brown." Everyone except Polly, that was.

Having had more than her fill of the smoke, the out-of-tune bellowing and the stink of beer, Polly decided to ride back to the house on her own. Although it was getting dark now, she knew the road well enough to ride without lights, and in any case the moon was out. She just wanted to be on her own for a while and enjoy her misery.

She let the pub door swing behind her, shutting off the noise as she stepped out into the quiet car park. She'd left her bicycle with the others leaning against the back fence, away from where the Yanks parked their Jeeps.

She rounded the corner of the pub and had to pick her way through the vehicles to get to the fence. As she did so, she heard a scuffling sound off to her left, then a bunch of hissing that sounded like steam gushing from a boiling kettle.

She stopped dead, wondering what could have caused the noise. Voices, low and muffled drifted across the silent Jeeps. Curious now, Polly crept toward the sound, bent almost double to avoid being seen by whoever was making the peculiar noise.

More scuffling, closer this time, brought her to a halt. The hissing noise sounded again, and she realized it was coming from the Jeep right in front of her. Carefully she peered around the bonnet.

There were three of them, all wearing handkerchiefs over their noses like the bank robbers she saw in the cowboy films. As she watched, she saw moonlight glinting on something in the nearest bloke's hand. It was a knife, and to her horror she saw him plunge it into one of the tires.

She drew back, terrified of being caught nosing. She'd heard about the gang from London and the damage they'd done in the village. She never expected to see them in the act.

Frantically she wondered what to do. She should go back to the pub and tell someone they were out there cutting up the tires on the Jeeps. But if they saw her, Gawd knows what they'd do to her. She felt sick at the thought.

In any case, by the time she got back to the pub, they'd be off and running anyway. It wasn't worth risking her life. She'd just have to wait until they were gone.

Squatting down behind the bonnet of the Jeep, she tried not to think about the pain in her knees. It seemed hours before they moved off. By that time they'd cut every one of the tires on every Jeep in the car park. Eight of them all told. Looked as if the Yanks would be walking home.

Just before the masked men left one of them chalked a message on the wall of the pub. Polly saw them running out of the car park and down the road. Even though her knees hurt and her legs were cramping, she waited until their footsteps had faded away into silence before she crept out from her hiding place.

She hobbled over to the pub to see what they'd scribbled on the wall. It was a message she'd seen a lot already. *Yanks go home!* And underneath, three distinct Ms, linked together. The three musketeers had been at work again.

Chapter 5

"Did you find Martin's glasses yet?" Elizabeth asked the next morning. She sat at the kitchen table, waiting for Violet to finish stirring the stodgy porridge that had become a regular offering for weekday breakfast. With eggs and bacon rationed, that particular treat was reserved for Sunday breakfast.

Now and again Violet managed to buy some smoked haddock, but Elizabeth didn't care for it without the customary poached eggs on top, and reluctantly settled on the porridge as a way to fill her stomach until the more palatable lunchtime menu.

"Can't find hide nor hair of them," Violet announced, as she dished up the steaming oatmeal onto the remaining china plates that were part of the second best service. "I sent Sadie all over the house looking for them. I'll have Polly help look for them today. Sadie won't go up into the attic rooms by herself. Not that I think that old goat climbed the stairs to the attic, but you never know with him nowadays."

"I thought the attic doors were locked," Elizabeth murmured. She was glancing at the headlines, disturbed to see the announcement that the Allies were expected to invade Sicily, and that bombing raids had already begun. As always, her thoughts were on Earl, and how involved he would be in the campaign.

"They are, but you know Martin has a set of keys to all the doors. I think we should take them away from him. Heaven knows what he's been up to lately."

"I don't think that's really necessary, do you?"

Violet dumped the plate of porridge in front of her. "I think we should lock him in his room, but I suppose that's too much to ask."

Elizabeth tore her gaze away from the newspaper. "Why? Has something happened?"

"I wondered when you were going to pay attention to me." Violet glanced up at the clock. "Where is he, that's what I want to know. He knows what time I serve breakfast. If he can't get here on time he doesn't deserve to eat it."

The door swung open at that instant and Martin shuffled slowly into the kitchen.

Violet gave him a sharp look. "Where the bloody hell have you been?"

"Good morning, madam," Martin said, pausing by Elizabeth's chair. "May I be permitted to join you at the table?"

"You certainly may, Martin." Elizabeth smiled at the old man. He looked so different without his glasses perched on his nose. "I see you haven't found your glasses yet."

"I haven't?" Martin fumbled at his forehead

with shaky fingers. "Bless my soul, no wonder I can't see to tie my shoelaces."

Obviously irritated at being totally ignored, Violet snapped, "You never look through them anyway, you old goat. You see just as well without them. I don't know why you bother to wear them at all."

"Perhaps you should try wearing spectacles yourself," Martin said huffily. "Then perhaps that fuzz on top of your head would look more like real hair and less like a bird's nest."

Violet looked taken aback. "What's got into you, this morning? Bit liverish, aren't we?"

Sensing another noisy argument brewing, Elizabeth said firmly, "I have to go into the village this morning, Violet. Could you please tell Polly to finish writing out the rent notices, and there's two letters that need answering. Rita Crumm is organizing a scavenger hunt. Most likely some members of the Housewives League will be calling on us to contribute."

"Contribute what?" Violet demanded. "What have you let us in for this time, Lizzie?"

"A scavenger hunt?" Martin looked horrified. "I trust those infernal housewives won't be tramping all over the house, madam? The master will be most displeased. He is upset enough as it is with all the comings and goings of our guests. He told me he is worried that what with all the strangers in the Manor House, an enemy spy could infiltrate and we'd never know he was here."

"Listen to him," Violet said with disgust. She slapped a plate of porridge in front of him. "Blinking barmy he is. What on earth would an enemy spy want with us?"

"I can't imagine," Martin said, rather dryly. "But I do suppose one of those blighters might be rather interested in the Americans."

"He has a point." Elizabeth patted his hand. "Don't worry, Martin, I'm sure we'd know if a stranger happened to be wandering around the Manor House."

"I fail to see how if I'm not wearing my glasses." Martin shook his head. "Anyone could sneak by me. The girl with the saucy mouth does it all the time."

Elizabeth looked inquiringly at Violet.

"Sadie," she said, shaking her head. "I have to admit, that girl gives him the devil of a time."

"Well, don't worry, Martin." Elizabeth reached for her cup of tea. "I'll have Polly and Sadie look for your glasses today. I'm sure we'll find them somewhere."

"He's probably flushed them down the lavatory," Violet said. "Wouldn't put anything past him." She tilted her head on one side and peered at the unfortunate butler. "Didn't exchange them for a bunch of raffle tickets, did you?"

Martin blinked at her in owlish innocence. "Raffle tickets?"

Violet picked up Elizabeth's half empty plate and tipped the remaining porridge into the sink.

"You know what I mean. All those raffle tickets you got hidden away in your drawers."

"How do you know what I have in my drawers?"

"I saw them when I was looking for your glasses." Violet swished water around the sink, and it gurgled noisily down the drain. "You keep buying them off that woman. What's her name? That Carr woman."

"If you are referring to Beatrice," Martin said coldly, "I'll thank you to refer to her as Mrs. Carr."

Violet sniffed. "Don't get all hoity-toity with me, you old fool. I don't know what you've been up to, Martin Chezzlewit, but I do know it can't be much good. Buying raffle tickets indeed. Whatever next? Bet you don't even know what's being raffled. I should think you'd have better things to do with your money. If you ask me, that woman is only after what she can get, you mind my words."

"Mrs. Carr happens to be a very charming lady." Martin put down his fork, dabbed his mouth with his serviette, then struggled painfully to his feet. "Which is far more than I can say about some people in this room." He nodded at Elizabeth. "Present company excluded, madam."

"Thank you, Martin." Elizabeth caught Violet's eye and gave her a swift shake of her head.

Violet snapped her mouth shut and turned back to the stove.

Martin leaned his gnarled hands on the table. "May I have the horse and carriage brought around for you, madam? Or will you be riding that dreadful mechanical monster?"

"I'll be taking the motorcycle, thank you, Martin." Elizabeth had long ago given up trying to convince her butler they no longer owned any horses, having sold them to help out with the mounting debts.

"Well, all I can say, I sincerely hope the master doesn't catch you astride that infernal machine. He would be aghast. Can't say I'd blame him."

"I can promise you, my father will not see me," Elizabeth assured him.

"Not unless he can see you from the grave," Violet muttered. She waited until Martin had shuffled slowly from the room before adding, "Did Rita say what her members would be looking for?"

"Not specifically, no." Elizabeth got to her feet. "Just common everyday knick-knacks I assume. The sort of things one has lying about. I suspect that none of them know what they will be asking for until they actually get the list. Otherwise it wouldn't be fair, would it."

"I don't know what we'd have lying about that they could want." Violet carried the empty porridge pot over to the sink. "If you ask me, they could find more useful things to do than waste our day with their silly games. I don't have time to hunt for what they want, and neither does Sadie."

"I wouldn't waste much time on it." Elizabeth headed for the door. "If you can't lay your hands on an item then simply tell them we don't have it."

She left Violet still grumbling to herself and closed the door on her housekeeper. Sometimes Violet could have quite a dampening effect on the day.

On the way to the stables, where she housed her motorcycle, Elizabeth spotted Desmond, the gardener, pruning the rosebushes behind the fountain. She hailed him, and waited for him to amble over to her. Like most of the men left in Sitting Marsh, Desmond was elderly and somewhat ineffective, but he kept the grounds under control, and was willing to accept a mere pittance for doing so, and for that Elizabeth forgave him a lot.

He came trudging up to her, pulling a shabby cap from his head as he reached her. "Morning, m'm. Looks like it be a nice day, today."

Glancing at the sparse clouds scudding across the sky on the wings of a fresh sea breeze, Elizabeth murmured, "I certainly hope so, Desmond."

"Going out are we, m'm?"

"Yes, Desmond. I'm going into the village, but I wanted to ask you something before I left."

Desmond's heavily wrinkled face took on a look of dismay. "Not going to ask me to tinker with your motorcycle, are you, m'm? Don't know much about engines, I don't. Grew up

with horses, you see. Now I could tell you anything you wanted to know about cart horses —"

"No, thank you, Desmond, it's not about my
motorcycle." Elizabeth glanced over at the
bushes growing on either side of the stone steps
that led to the front door. "What do you know
about daphne?"

Desmond's brow wrinkled even deeper.
"Daphne? Don't know as I'm acquainted with
anyone of that name, m'm."

"No, it's not a person," Elizabeth said patiently. "I'm talking about those bushes over
there." She pointed to the dark green leaves
sprinkled with delicate pink flowers. "Isn't that
daphne?"

"Oh, is it, m'm?" Desmond stared at it for a
moment or two. "Wouldn't know the name of
it, m'm, but I do know you can't eat them orange berries on it. Got some juice from them
on me fingers once, and wiped me mouth
without thinking. Burned me lips like acid it
did. Never go near them bushes now without
me gloves."

"So it doesn't seem likely that anyone would
actually eat the berries, then?"

"Not unless they want to burn their guts out.
Begging your pardon, m'm, but I can't see
anyone actually swallowing them things. Bitter
as drain cleaner they be."

Elizabeth frowned. "More so than bitter ale or
stout, would you say?"

Desmond gave her a wide display of uneven

yellowed teeth. "Depends how much you have of it, m'm, if you get my meaning."

"Yes, I suppose so." Elizabeth pulled a rose-pink silk scarf from the pocket of her cardigan and arranged it over her hat, tying both ends securely under her chin. "Well, I'm off. Thank you, Desmond. I must say, you are doing an excellent job with the roses."

"Thank you, m'm." Desmond gave her a quaint, old-fashioned bow from the waist, then hobbled back to his task.

Elizabeth sighed. How she missed the skilled gardeners and maintenance men that once kept the manor and its grounds in sparkling order. Most of them were in the military now, of course, but in the aftermath of her parents' death and her subsequent divorce, she'd had to sack the remaining staff. All but Violet and Martin. Polly and Sadie were recent additions, and she could barely afford them.

So much needed to be done in the house. She and Violet had managed makeshift repairs, with the help of Desmond and in spite of the hindrance of Martin who, more often than not, insisted on giving a hand.

They'd cleaned chimneys and repaired lighting fixtures, hung blackout curtains and unplugged lavatories. So far, however, they hadn't managed to solve the problem of loudly gurgling water pipes, or the occasional leaks in the roof during a heavy downpour.

Earl had found a young man at the base who

had training as a plumber but the poor fellow, when faced with an alarming array of ancient pipes and an antiquated system that ran throughout the vast manor, had confessed that the task was far beyond his capabilities, and suggested Elizabeth call in an experienced plumber.

All very well said and done, Elizabeth thought, as she wheeled her motorcycle out of the stables. But the only plumber to be found in the village was serving in the navy somewhere in the Pacific, and being able to afford a competent plumber from North Horsham was out of the question.

So the pipes merrily gurgled, groaned and hissed away, no doubt giving rise to the persistent rumors that the Manor House was haunted by its previous inhabitants. Including her own father and mother.

Elizabeth thought about her parents as she sped down the hill toward the main street of Sitting Marsh. She missed them both dreadfully, and at times her sense of loss was almost overwhelming.

Taking over the sprawling mansion and its vast acres of land was difficult enough, but inheriting the title of lady of the manor, sole heir of the last earl of Wellsborough, had been daunting at times. Especially since it was common knowledge in the village that the late earl's wife had been nothing more than a kitchen maid when he married her. Elizabeth's claim to aristocracy had been severely hampered by that fact. At least to some people. Rita Crumm in particular.

Her thoughts on the impending scavenger hunt, Elizabeth roared down the high street, graciously acknowledging the scattered villagers on the street by returning their waves with a quick flick of her wrist.

Her sparse response was necessitated by her need to hang onto the handlebars with both hands. Much as she enjoyed the stir she caused when entering the village on her mechanical steed, she had no wish to crash the darn thing and end up with her feet in the air and her skirts around her head. Rita Crumm would feast on that spectacle for the rest of her born days. Thanks to the sidecar, which helped maintain her balance, the chance of that happening was remote. Unless she lost control of the vehicle, of course.

Thankfully coming to a halt in front of the police station, Elizabeth shut off her engine and climbed off the saddle. She wanted a word with the constables before she rode out to the Adelaides' dairy farm. Not that she expected any real help from them, but it wouldn't hurt to let them know she was helping with the enquiries. That way she could defend herself should the police inspector make a rare visit and accuse her of intruding in police work.

Police Constable George Dalrymple was seated at his desk as usual when she entered, a huge bag of pastries from Bessie's bake shop sitting in front of him. One hand held a Banbury cake with a huge bite taken out of it, and George's jaws worked at the piece in his mouth as he rose to his feet.

"Goo' morn'n your ladyship," he mumbled, and dabbed at his mouth with a large white handkerchief. "Just having me elevenses, like. Can I offer you a currant bun?"

Elizabeth glanced at the clock above his head. The hands pointed at twenty to ten, but she refrained from pointing out that George was a trifle early to be enjoying elevenses. "No thank you, George, I've just eaten a bowl of porridge. But I do appreciate the offer."

"Not at all, m'm." George waved a pudgy hand at a vacant chair. "Please have a seat, won't you?"

Elizabeth sat, pulling her skirt well down over her knees.

George cleared his throat. "I was just saying to Sid, as how I thought that was your motorcycle making that rack . . . er . . . noise outside. Weren't I, Sid?"

This last was bellowed for the benefit of George's beleaguered partner, P.C. Sid Goffin, who had apparently been relegated to the back room.

Sid's voice wafted out from behind the open door. "That's right, your ladyship. George was saying what a blasted racket it made."

"Yes, well, right," George said loudly and

hastily. "What can we do for your ladyship this fine morning?"

"I hope you're not scoffing down them cakes," Sid shouted from the back room. "I don't want to come out at eleven o'clock and find them all gone."

George's cheeks turned red and he brushed his mouth with the back of his hand. "Take no notice of 'im," he said, jerking his head in the direction of the door. "Never has a civil tongue in his head until he's had his tea and crumpets."

Sid said something that Elizabeth couldn't catch, which was just as well if George's embarrassed expression was anything to go by.

Saving the poor man from having to make amends for Sid's insolence, she said quickly, "Actually, George, I stopped by to ask about the doctor who operated on the Adelaides' daughter, Barbara. I —"

"How did you hear about that then?" George demanded, sounding a little belligerent.

"Mrs. Adelaide told me." Elizabeth fixed him with a stern look. "I trust the matter is under investigation?"

George looked hurt. "The inspector is looking into it, yes."

"Very good." Elizabeth settled back in her chair. "Has he made any headway in the case?"

"I wouldn't know about that, your ladyship. And even if I did, I —"

"Yes, I know. You wouldn't be at liberty to discuss it with me. In that case, perhaps you can tell me what you've heard about the recent deaths of the American airmen. Some kind of poisoning, I understand."

George's expression immediately turned wary. "Poison?"

"Poison," Elizabeth said firmly. "Four of them died from it. I was sure you'd heard about it."

George reached for a pencil and began tapping the end of it on the desk. "Well, now, maybe I 'ave and maybe I 'aven't."

"Do stop being coy with me, George. I don't have time to play games. Do you or do you not know anything about these unfortunate incidents?"

George scratched his balding pate. "Well, m'm, I heard something, but I don't rightly know what to make of it. Some say it were a mysterious sickness that's going around, some foreign germs what the Yanks brought over from America." George squinted his eyes almost shut. "They got lots of germs over there, m'm. Come from the swamps and the deserts they do."

"Yes, well, I'm quite sure we have just as many germs here." Elizabeth smoothed the fingers of her gloves. "Actually I heard that the poison came from a plant. Daphne, to be exact."

George looked puzzled. "Who's Daphne?"

"It's a plant, George. It grows in people's gardens. It has pretty little flowers and orange berries that can make you very, very sick. The doctors at the base think the Americans may have eaten the berries."

"Go on! So that's how they died. Silly buggers. Probably got drunk and thought they were cherries or something."

"Perhaps." Elizabeth paused, then added carefully, "What do you know about the three musketeers?"

The wary expression returned. "Weren't they some kind of highwaymen in the old days?"

"Not exactly. But in any case, I wasn't talking about those musketeers. I was talking about the three men who apparently travel down from London intent on committing crimes against the Americans."

"What kind of crimes?"

Elizabeth sighed. "You know very well what I'm talking about George. Damage to the Jeeps, that sort of thing."

"She's talking about the lads what cut the tires on all those Jeeps last night," Sid called out helpfully.

Elizabeth sat up straight, while George looked as if he were about to rush in and strangle his partner.

"Last night? Those men were here last night?"

"Yes, m'm. I'm afraid they were." George stood up. "I'm sorry, your ladyship, but I can't say no more. Sid shouldn't have told you that much but you know what he's like." He sent a glowering glance at the door. "Can't keep his blinking mouth shut for a minute, he can't."

"What'd I say?" Sid demanded from the back room.

"Just give me a blinking minute and I'll be in there to tell you what you said!" George cleared his throat again and lowered his voice. "Beg your pardon, m'm, but that's all I can say right now."

"You don't have any clues as to their identities?" Elizabeth got to her feet.

"None at all, m'm. No one seems to know what they look like."

"But you would tell me if you had something to go on?"

George looked uncomfortable. "I'll tell you what I can, m'm. That's all I can promise."

"Very well, George. I suppose that will have to do."

"I'd ask young Polly if I were you, your ladyship," Sid piped up.

Elizabeth paused at the door. "Polly?"

"If you don't blinking shut up I'll shove your teeth right down your bloomin' throat!" George roared.

"Thank you, Sid. Good day to you both." Elizabeth stepped outside and took a deep breath of the fresh warm air. *Polly*. She had no idea what her young assistant had to do with anything but she was certainly going to find out.

Chapter 6

"Now," Rita Crumm said, when she was sure she had everyone's attention. "Have you all got the list of items in front of you?"

Florrie Evans, a thin wisp of a woman with a nervous twitch to her nose, held up a trembling hand.

Rita inwardly cursed. If anyone was going to mess things up, trust Florrie to be in the front of the line. The woman never got anything straight, and when she did, she usually forgot it again before she could make use of it. "What is it, Florrie?" she demanded testily. "Didn't you get a list?"

"Yes, I did," Florrie said, her quavery voice jarring Rita's nerves. "I just wanted to ask if we can get more than one thing from one place."

"You can get them all from one place if you can find them." Rita sniffed, and resisted the urge to swipe at her own nose with the back of her hand. Watching Florrie's nose twitch like that made her itch. "It's up to you. But if I were you, I wouldn't go asking people for the whole list at once. They're likely to tell you where to put it."

Florrie looked puzzled. "Where do I put it, then?"

Marge Gunther giggled, and jabbed Maisie Parsons in the arm with her elbow.

"Ouch," Maisie muttered. "That hurt."

A young girl spoke up from the back of the room. "Can we go to the American base to get some things on the list?"

Nellie Smith was young, pretty, and unmarried. Rita secretly envied all three, and barely tolerated the woman. It was well known in the village that Nellie had more boyfriends at the base than fleas on a dog's back. Rita envied her that, too. "I don't think they'd look too kindly on us if we go pestering the boys at the base for a scavenger hunt," she said scathingly. "I'd think they have more important things to take care of out there."

"Yeah, Nellie," Marge called out. "You can't go asking the Yanks for their combinations. You'd get thrown in the clink."

"Don't be daft," Nellie said, with a touch of scorn. "Everyone knows Yanks don't wear 'em."

Shrill jeers and cheers greeted this comment. "Only Nellie would know that Yanks don't wear underpants," Marge said with a grin.

"I didn't say they didn't wear underpants," Nellie protested. "I said as how they don't wear combs."

"What do they wear then?" someone else asked.

"Never you mind."

"Whatever it is they wear, it wouldn't be on them long with Nellie around," Marge said.

"You're only jealous." Nellie flicked her hair back with her fingers. "You're all jealous, the lot of you."

Marge laughed. "Not me. I'm too old to mess around with Yanks. Give me my old man anytime. He might have snow on the roof but he's still got a fire in the fireplace."

More whoops and cheers followed.

Rita held up her hand. "That's enough! We're not here to discuss the Americans, we're here to organize the scavenger hunt. So let's get on with it."

"I think we should have nylons on the list," Nellie said, in open defiance. "That way we'd get a little something for ourselves as well."

"You'll get more than nylons one of these days, my girl," Maisie said, surprising everyone. Maisie Parsons rarely spoke up unless spoken to first. "Them Yanks'll be the death of you. Nothing but trouble, they are. Stay away from them if you want my advice."

"They were good enough for Pauline, though, weren't they," Nellie muttered.

"You leave my granddaughter out of it," Maisie snapped back. "She soon learned what they're like and you will, too. Only by then it'll be too late."

Faces turned in Maisie's direction, while Nellie asked the question on everyone's mind. "Your Pauline in trouble then, is she?"

" 'Course not," Maisie said hastily. "She went back to London to be with her old boyfriend,

91

that's all. But if she hadn't played around with the Yanks down here and got her heart broken, she wouldn't have gone back and left me all alone. She'd still be here safe with me instead of living in London with all them bombs. I'm afraid that any day now I'll hear as how she got killed in a bombing raid."

There were murmurs of sympathy in response to this dampening speech.

Rita sighed. She couldn't stand to lose control of a situation and right now it seemed as if no one in the room was listening to her. It was time to get their attention. "If you all want to be back in time for afternoon tea you'd better get a bloody move on!" she yelled.

Everyone stopped talking and looked at her. Having successfully regained the focus of interest, she continued in a milder tone. "It's almost eleven o'clock. You have until three o'clock this afternoon. That's four hours to get as much on the list as possible. The one who gets the most on the list gets the prize."

"What's the prize?" Marge asked, her beady eyes gleaming with excitement.

Rita leaned over and reached for the basket hidden behind her chair. "This is the prize." She held up the basket, which had been gaily decorated with her daughter Lilly's hair ribbons. "I'm going to need the basket and the ribbons back," she announced, "but you can keep what's inside."

"What's inside it, then?" Marge persisted.

Rita put the basket on her lap and reached inside. "There's a bottle of lavender water," she held it up, "and two clothing coupons, a packet of lemonade powder, six pieces of Maisie's gingerbread . . ." she paused until the enthusiastic murmurs died down ". . . and *this!*" With a flourish she withdrew a cellophane package and waved it in the air.

"Nylons!" Nellie screamed. "How'd you get them?"

"My Lilly got them. Never mind how." Rita tucked them back into the basket amid a chorus of questions. Ignoring them all, she raised her voice above the clamor. "Now get going. You can work together if you want to, but you'll do better on your own. It's up to you. We'll meet back at Bessie's bake shop for afternoon tea at three. Anyone who's more than five minutes late will be disqualified. Everyone got that?"

Chattering with anticipation, the women hustled out of the door, leaving Rita alone in the blessed peace of her living room. One more great event launched. She jiggled the basket on her lap. And if that Nellie Smith thought she was going to get her dirty little hands on the basket she was in for a huge disappointment. Somehow, Rita promised herself, she'd make sure the precious prize would go to someone who deserved it. Like poor Maisie, worrying about her granddaughter, or even fluttery Florrie, who never won anything in her life.

Anyone other than that smarmy, know-it-all Nellie.

Content with that for the moment, Rita stashed the basket in a kitchen cupboard, and sat down to work out her next great event.

Dark clouds had begun gathering by the time Elizabeth reached the dairy farm. She wished she'd worn her macintosh coat, since it looked very much as if it were about to rain. One got so dreadfully soaked while riding a motorcycle in the rain.

She coasted down the road toward the Adelaides' cottage and mindful of the noise, turned off her engine a few yards before she reached the gate. She really didn't want to have to explain why she was interested in the garden. If Dick Adelaide was responsible for the poisoning, it wouldn't do to let him know she suspected him of picking berries in his garden in order to kill innocent young men.

The sun disappeared behind a black cloud as she walked slowly toward the wooden gate. All along the fence marigolds grew in thick orange clusters, and beyond them a neat square of lawn spread out in front of the cottage.

Elizabeth spotted hydrangea bushes beneath the latticed windows, almost hidden by tall, swaying hollyhocks and white Canterbury bells. There was no sign of daphne shrubs anywhere.

With her gaze on the ground in front of her, Elizabeth walked around the side of the house.

A tall fence prevented her from seeing inside the back garden, but a rickety gate in the center had been left unlatched.

The wind could well blow it open, Elizabeth reasoned, giving it a tiny push to help it along. Unfortunately something seemed to be obstructing the gate, and she had to give it quite a hefty shove to get it open wide enough to poke her head through.

She peered around the edge of the gate and received a nasty shock. Annie Adelaide stood on the other side, staring at her in disbelief, one hand holding what appeared to be a pair of knickers, while the other held a wooden clothes peg. At a short distance from her feet a basket lay sprawled on its side, and some of its contents had spilled out.

Elizabeth realized now what had been obstructing the gate. It was a basket of clean wash, most of which now lay in the grass. "Oh," she said faintly, "I'm most dreadfully sorry."

Annie looked down at the scattered clothes and murmured, "It's all right, your ladyship. I don't think they got all that dirty."

Feeling utterly mortified, Elizabeth pushed through the gate and righted the basket. She began picking up the pieces of laundry, shaking them out before replacing them in the basket. All the time her mind was racing, searching for an excuse for her inexcusable behavior.

"That's all right, m'm. Just leave it. I'll see to it."

95

Dropping an undershirt into the basket, Elizabeth rose, uncomfortably aware of her burning face. "I do apologize, Mrs. Adelaide. The truth is, I lost my scarf yesterday and I was wondering if I'd left it here when I came to visit. I knocked on the door but you must not have heard me."

Annie Adelaide stared pointedly at the scarf that held down Elizabeth's hat.

"It was a blue scarf," Elizabeth mumbled.

"Ah, well, I'm afraid you didn't leave it here, m'm." Annie dropped the knickers into the basket, then turned to unpeg the next garment. "I'm sure I would have noticed it if you had."

"Yes, well, I suppose I must have left it somewhere else. I'm so sorry to have bothered you."

"Quite all right, m'm. Can I offer you some tea?"

"No, thank you," Elizabeth said hurriedly. "I really don't have time to stay." Fighting the urge to turn tail and run, she made herself look around. "My, what a pretty garden you have! So many flowers!"

"I like flowers," Annie said, a trifle defensively. "I pick them and put them in the house. Makes it smell fresh and clean."

"Yes, I suppose it does." Elizabeth pointed to a lush display of white daisies. "How pretty. I do love daisies." She walked over to them, conscious of Annie's eyes boring into her back. "And what is this?" She pointed to a small shrub covered in fragile pink blossoms.

There seemed to be a significant pause before

Annie answered. "I believe it's called wood laurel, m'm. Though some people do call it daphne."

"Yes," Elizabeth murmured. "I thought so." She twisted around to find Annie staring at her with an odd expression on her face. "Well, I must be getting along. I'm so sorry about the wash. I do hope you won't have to wash it all again."

"Don't worry about it, your ladyship. No harm done."

"Well, thank you." Smiling and nodding, Elizabeth escaped through the gate. She practically ran back to her motorcycle, feeling all the time as if Annie Adelaide's fierce gaze were burning into her back.

It wasn't so much the sight of the daphne that bothered her so. After all, lots of people grew the fragrant shrub in their gardens, and that didn't necessarily mean that someone was guilty of murder.

On the other hand, what had upset her so was the fact that despite peering as hard as she could at the flowering shrub, she hadn't see one single berry nestled among its deadly dark green leaves. Which led her to wonder exactly what had happened to them.

Polly sat in the office, staring at the stack of rental notices without much interest. It was a boring job, and she usually put it off as long as possible. All those cottages, all sitting on the land belonging to Lady Elizabeth. It blew her mind. By rights her ladyship should be rolling in money, instead of having to juggle the bills every month. It didn't seem right.

Not that it was any of her business, of course. The first thing Lady Elizabeth had done when she'd hired her as her assistant was make her promise not to discuss the business of the manor with anyone. It wouldn't do for word to get out in the village that the lady of the manor, the woman everyone looked up to and respected, was just as poor off as they were and couldn't afford a plumber to fix the water pipes.

If there was one thing Polly prided herself for, it was her ability to keep her mouth shut. She was proud of being trusted with such an enormous secret, and nothing and nobody would be able to pry it out of her. Not even Sam.

The door opened and Polly jumped, expecting to see her ladyship come sailing through the door. It was Sadie's cheerful face, however, grinning at her from the doorway.

"Watcha doing?" Sadie came into the office, gazing around her as if she'd never been in there before. "Seems to me this place could use some sprucing up. You don't even have a calendar on the wall."

"Don't need one," Polly said, shuffling the pile of papers in front of her in an effort to look like a hardworking assistant. "I don't need nothing on the wall to tell me what day it is."

"Maybe not, but they're nice to look at. I have

one in my room and I look forward to turning the page at the end of the month. It's like you got twelve different pictures to look at on your wall every year. Besides, every new picture I see reminds me it's one month closer to the end of the war."

Polly bit her tongue before she could say what was on her mind. She didn't want to admit that if she were really, truly honest with herself, she didn't want the war to end. Not yet, anyway. Because if it did, that would mean Sam would go back to America without her.

She needed time. Time to make him see what a terrible mistake it would be to leave her behind in England. They were meant to be together, and one day he was going to realize that. All she could hope was that he wouldn't wait until he got back home to find that out.

"Anyhow," Sadie said, shattering Polly's thoughts. "I was sent up here to ask you to help me find Martin's glasses."

"Didn't know they was lost." Polly started writing out the first rent notice. "Anyhow, I'm busy."

"Well, all right, then." Sadie turned toward the door. "But I thought you'd like to know the Yanks haven't left for the base yet. You could bump into Sam on the way up to the attic."

Polly's chin shot up. "The attic? Well, why didn't you say so!" She got up from her chair. "Though why would Martin's glasses be in the attic?"

Sadie snorted. "You're asking me why Martin does what he does? He's off his blinking rocker, isn't he. How the heck do I know why he does daft things? We've looked everywhere else in the house for them, and that's the last place to look."

Polly followed her out into the great hall. "Perhaps he lost 'em in the gardens."

"Violet says he never goes in the gardens. He's afraid of getting lost and not finding his way back."

"Lost in the gardens? He can see the house from there. It's blinking big enough."

Sadie shrugged. "Don't ask me. I'm only the flipping housemaid, aren't I. I do what I'm told and I don't ask questions. Vi says to look in the attic so I'm looking in the attic." She nudged Polly's arm. "Besides, attics are fun. You never know what you're going to find in there."

Polly looked at her in admiration. "You call her Vi?"

"Only when she's not listening." Sadie grinned. "Come on, let's get down the hall before the Yanks leave."

Seconds later, to Polly's intense disappointment, she heard the muffled roar of engines outside. "We're too late," she told Sadie. "They're leaving right now."

"Ah well, maybe it's just as well." Sadie unlocked the door that led to the attic stairs. "You only get upset whenever you see him, anyway."

"I get upset when I don't see him," Polly

grumbled. "And I don't see him a lot these days."

Sadie stood back. "All right, you go first."

Polly glanced up the stairs. It was dark up there, and smelled funny, like the coal cellar right after the coalman had left. "Why don't you go first?"

"Why'd you think I told Violet I needed you to help me?" Sadie shivered, clutching the collar of her blouse. "I'm not going up there first. That's what I brought you for."

"What're you afraid of? Ghosts?" Polly uttered a shaky laugh and started up the stairs. She tried not to think about the shadowy man she'd seen disappear into the curtains. Sam was right. It was all in her mind.

Sadie's stomping footsteps behind her were somewhat reassuring, but still Polly could feel her skin crawling as she reached the top of the stairs. It was so cold up there. And damp. And creepy.

Sadie reached her side, and peered around. "Vi said there are three rooms, all leading off each other."

"I've never been up here before." Polly ventured into the small room ahead of her. On one side the ceiling sloped so sharply it almost reached the floor. Opposite her was the tiny oval window that she could see from the outside. Crossing over to it, she looked down on the courtyard below. It seemed an awful long way down.

She could see the whole driveway from that window, and just caught a glimpse of the Jeeps before they rounded the bend and disappeared from view. Her heart ached. Another day without seeing Sam. Sometimes she didn't think she could bear it anymore.

"Gawd, look at this mess."

Polly turned to see Sadie on her knees in front of a big black trunk. The lid was thrown back and Sadie was lifting brightly colored paper chains in her hands.

"That's the old Christmas decorations," Polly said, moving closer to take a look at them. "They used them to decorate the town hall once, when they held a dance for the Yanks."

"Go on!" Sadie stared up at her. "Did they do the jitterbug and everything?"

"Yeah, they did." Polly smiled at the memory. "It was really smashing, dancing with Sam. Until our lads started scrapping with the Yanks. Then all hell broke loose."

"Blimey, what happened?"

"Well, some things got smashed up and Lady Elizabeth said she weren't going to do it no more." Polly sighed. "It's a shame, really. We was all having such a lovely time."

"Sounds like it. Maybe we can talk her into doing another one. Those pitiful dances they have at the church hall are a waste of bloomin' time. None of the Yanks go, nor our army blokes, neither."

"That's because they don't serve beer there."

Polly scanned the odd assortment of furniture, paintings, mysterious bundles and boxes with a frown. "We got to look through all this lot? It will take us weeks."

Sadie stood up and brushed her hands together. "Nah, just look really close and see if the dust has been disturbed. If it ain't, then we know Martin's never been up here to drop his glasses."

Polly squinted in the shadows. "Don't look like no one's been up here in a while."

"I can't see that old man hobbling up them steps anyway. This is a big bloomin' waste of time if you ask me." Sadie stomped across the floor, raising a small cloud of dust as she pulled open the door in the corner. Poking her head inside she muttered, "Gawd luvaduck. We'll never get in there, leave alone find anything. And if we can't, that means that old man never did, neither. Let's just say we looked and leave it at that." She shut the door, then sneezed violently, making Polly jump again.

"All right." Only too happy to get out of that creepy room, Polly turned to head for the steps. In her hurry, her knee banged into one of the boxes, sending it crashing to the floor.

Sadie let out a squeak. "Crikey, you nearly gave me a heart attack."

"Sorry." Polly squatted on her heels and turned the box upright. "Looks like a load of old photographs. They're all faded and brown." She held up a picture of an elegant woman wearing a large hat and a lace dress with a high collar and a skirt that fell to her ankles. "Look at this. Must be a hundred years old."

Sadie took it from her. "Nah, more like forty years. They didn't have a film camera a hundred years ago." She handed the picture back to Polly. "I'm glad I didn't live back then."

"Oh, I don't know." Polly studied the aged photograph. "It looks nice, sort of peaceful."

"Nah, you'd miss going to the pictures and seeing all your favorite film stars. Cary Grant wasn't even born back then." Sadie's foot struck something, and she bent over to pick it up. It was a small wooden casket, and by the way she was holding it, fairly heavy.

"Open it," Polly said. She dropped the photograph back in the box with the others and stacked it back on the pile.

Sadie prized the lid open, and sniffed. "Smells like roses." She reached inside and drew out a small pink package.

"What is it?" Polly scrambled to her feet. "Oo, it's got a lovely pong."

"It's scented soap," Sadie said, reading off the label. "Look, it's shaped like a rose." She tipped the casket toward the window so she could see the contents. "There's a lot of packages in here, all different soaps. There's lavender and lilac and . . . oo, what's that? Orange blossom?" Sadie picked up the pale peach packet and held it to her nose. "Smells like a tropical island."

"Let me smell!" Polly took the package from

her. Just as she did so, something caught her eye in the corner behind Sadie. It was the figure of a woman — a small, elegant woman wearing a big hat. Polly's blood ran cold as the figure actually *moved*.

She let out a shriek, dropped the package of soap and lunged for the steps. She went down them so fast her feet missed a couple of them, and she landed in a heap at the bottom.

Sadie came clattering down behind her, demanding, "What the bloody hell's the matter with you?"

"Ghost," Polly gasped. "Let's get out of here." Without waiting to see if Sadie followed, she flung herself through the door, belted down the great hall and didn't stop until she reached the office.

Chapter 7

Elizabeth looked up as Polly slammed through the office door at full tilt. The girl was as pale as chalk and looked about to faint dead away.

"Good heavens, Polly," Elizabeth exclaimed. "Whatever is the matter?"

"Ghost, m'm," Polly said, panting for breath. "In the attic. I saw her plain as the nose on me face." She flopped down on her chair and held both hands to the sides of her head. "Oh, m'm, it were awful."

Alarmed, Elizabeth said sharply, "Are you sure?" Then common sense took over. "Of course you didn't see a ghost. Polly, tell me exactly what you did see."

"A lady, like the one in the photograph. Oh . . . oo . . . oh, I'll never go up there again. Not if me life depended on it. I swear I won't."

"What photograph?"

Polly stopped shuddering and lowered her hands. "The one in the box. I knocked it over and these photographs fell out. One was of a lady in a long dress and a big hat and I saw her, I swear I did!"

"Calm down, Polly." Elizabeth wished she had a bottle of the smelling salts her mother always carried with her. "What you saw was probably the dressmaker's form up there. I distinctly remember seeing it when we were looking for decorations for the town hall."

Polly stared at her with wide eyes. "Were it wearing a long dress and a big hat?"

"Well, no," Elizabeth admitted, "but it's dark up there and shadows sometimes move. I've seen them myself. You probably imagined the hat and dress."

"Begging your pardon, m'm, but this weren't no shadow. I saw her. I saw her better half yesterday as well."

"Her better half?" Elizabeth repeated in bewilderment.

"Yes, m'm. He weren't in the photograph with her but I know it were him. He was dressed in old-fashioned clothes as well. Just like her."

"He was wearing a dress?"

Polly giggled, sounding a little hysterical. "No, m'm, he were wearing a suit. And a bowler hat."

Elizabeth sighed. "Polly, I can assure you, if there were ghosts in the Manor House, I'm quite sure I'd know about them."

"Yes, m'm," Polly said, quite meekly, though her expression clearly stated she was not convinced.

"I assume you didn't find Martin's glasses?"

Polly started, as if she'd forgotten until that moment the reason she was in the attic in the first place. "Oh, no, m'm. We didn't. Me and

107

Sadie looked all over, but if you ask me I don't think anyone's been up in that attic since Christmas. Except the ghosts, that is. They don't mess up the dust, do they."

Deciding it was time to change the subject, Elizabeth said briskly, "Well, I wanted to ask you something. I was down at the police station today and Sid mentioned your name. He seemed to think you know something about a group of men from London called the three musketeers."

Polly looked worried. "Well, I wouldn't say I know anything about them. I have heard of them though. Just about everyone in the village has heard of them." She hesitated, then added in a rush, "But I did see them last night. Down at the Tudor Arms. Or in the car park, rather. When I went back and told Alfie, he rang P.C. Dalrymple."

"Ah, so that's what Sid was talking about. Can you describe the men to me?"

"Not really, m'm." She gave a decisive shake of her head. "They wore handkerchiefs over their noses and I didn't get a really good look at them. Except . . ." Again she paused.

"Except?" Elizabeth prompted.

"Well, they was young. I mean they weren't old men. I could tell by their voices, and the way they moved."

"Could you tell what color hair they had?"

"I can't say as I noticed," Polly said slowly. "Just ordinary color hair, I s'pose."

"Was anyone else with you when you saw them?"

"No, m'm. I left the pub early. Marlene and Sadie were there and Sadie was singing in the talent contest. I was getting tired of all the noise. I was on me way back to me bicycle when I heard a weird noise in the car park. I saw three men cutting the tires on the Jeeps with a big knife. I hid until they ran off. Oh, and I saw them scribble words on the wall of the pub."

"Do you remember seeing them inside the pub earlier?"

Polly shook her head. "They might have been, I s'pose, but I don't remember seeing them there."

"What about the clothes they wore? Think hard, Polly. You must remember something."

Polly screwed up her face in an effort to remember, then said unhappily, "I'm sorry, m'm. It were getting dark, and I was too scared to notice much about them."

Elizabeth sighed. "All right, Polly. Thank you. Now finish these rent notices, will you? We must deliver them to the post office tomorrow."

"Yes, m'm." Polly drew her chair closer to her desk and reached for the inkstand. "There's a lot here, m'm."

"Well, do the best you can. It's almost lunchtime, so you'll have to finish this afternoon." Elizabeth got up and headed for the door. "I have some errands to run later, but if you haven't finished by the time I get back I'll give you a hand."

Polly gave her a sweet smile. "Thank you, m'm. That's really nice of you."

Elizabeth left, reflecting on how pretty the child was when she smiled, and that it was a pity Polly didn't smile more often. Probably moping over that nice young squadron leader, no doubt. Such a shame. So many heartaches in wartime romances. Including her own. Depressed at the thought, she made her way to the kitchen.

Sadie was there when she entered, talking earnestly to Violet, who was busy at the stove as usual. Martin sat at the table, staring in front of him at a box of what appeared to be tablets of scented soap, judging by the strong fragrance.

"I don't know what it was," Sadie said, as the door closed behind Elizabeth, "but it scared the shit out of Polly."

Martin caught sight of Elizabeth at that moment and struggled to his feet. "Good morning, Lady Elizabeth. You're rather late for breakfast, are you not?"

Sadie swung around, while Violet muttered, "We had breakfast hours ago, you old fool. It's almost time for lunch."

"I'm glad to hear it," Elizabeth said. "I'm absolutely famished." She sat down at the table and reached for the box. "What's this?"

"We found it in the attic, m'm," Sadie said, moving closer to the table. "I thought, what with the shortage of good soap, it might come in useful."

Elizabeth picked up a packet and sniffed deeply. "My, it does smell good."

"That's what I was telling Violet," Sadie said with relish. "It's got a bloody good pong to it. It would turn a few heads at the Arms, I can tell you."

Martin tutted in disgust. "Young lady, I'll thank you to use proper language when addressing her ladyship. Please save that disgusting vernacular for that ghastly den of iniquity the likes of you are so fond of patronizing."

Sadie grinned at him. "Aw, Martin, you don't know what you're missing. You should come down the pub on a Sunday night when we're all singing around the piano. I bet you could show 'em a thing or two, right?"

Martin sniffed. "I wouldn't be caught dead in that miserable hole. Nothing but drunken louts and fast women."

"See, I told you it was fun." She nudged Martin hard in the arm, almost knocking him off his feet. "Oh, sorry, mate. Keep forgetting you're a bit unsteady on your pins."

Martin grasped the back of his chair for support and drew himself up as far as he was able, which wasn't very far. "If you dare lay a finger on me again, young lady, and I use the term with a great deal of margin, I shall be forced to remove you from the premises."

Sadie stuck her face close to his. "You'd miss me, luv, you know you would."

Noticing Martin's face turning purple, Elizabeth decided it was time to intervene. "Thank you for bringing down the soap, Sadie," she said loudly. "It will make a pleasant change from that dreadful stuff we get from the chemist." She reached for a packet and handed it to Sadie. "Here, you can have this. I'll give one to Polly when she comes down for lunch."

"Thank you, m'm." Sadie took the soap from her and held it to her nose. "Scented soap. What a treat. This will make me feel like a proper lady."

"There isn't anything on this earth that could possibly help you in the least resemble a lady," Martin said nastily.

"Sadie," Violet said sharply, "stop tormenting Martin and come and mash these potatoes for me."

"Well, all right." Sadie slipped the soap in her apron pocket. "But it's not nearly as much fun."

Martin grunted something under his breath, then in a completely different tone asked, "May I be permitted to join you at the table, madam?"

"Certainly, Martin." Elizabeth glanced at the clock. "Polly will be down any minute. Then we can all have lunch."

"Disgraceful, that's what I call it," Martin mumbled.

Elizabeth wasn't sure to what he was referring, but wisely decided to ignore the comment. With any luck, they would get through the meal without any more bickering.

To her relief her hopes were realized, and she enjoyed a pleasant meal with her staff at the spacious kitchen table. Although both Martin and Violet had loudly voiced their doubts in the past on the wisdom of sharing her meals with the servants, Elizabeth had insisted, having formed a violent distaste for eating in the vast dining room alone.

On occasion Earl joined her for supper there, and then it was an immense pleasure, but otherwise she preferred to take her meals in the warm security of her kitchen, surrounded by the people she considered her family, complete with all the eccentricities and foibles one normally encountered with relatives.

With peace restored, the conversation throughout the meal was light-hearted. That was, until Sadie recounted the night's events at the pub, and described in great detail the wrath of the GIs when they discovered their tires in shreds. A lorry had to be summoned from the base, bringing new tires that the men had to replace on their wheels, thus making them very late in returning to their beds.

"I don't suppose anyone noticed these men in the pub earlier," Elizabeth said, without much hope.

"Nobody knows what they look like." Sadie flicked a glance at Polly. "Polly's the only one what's seen 'em, and it was too dark for her to see what they looked like."

"If you'll excuse me, madam." Martin struggled to his feet, and stood gasping for breath for a moment or two.

"Of course, Martin." Elizabeth peered at the clock above the stove. "You're late for your nap today."

"Yes, madam. I can barely keep my eyes open. I'll take my leave now, with your permission?"

"Have a good rest." Elizabeth smiled at him.

"Thank you, madam." He shuffled slowly to the door, dragged it open, and disappeared through it. The door swung behind him, apparently a little faster than he'd anticipated, since a distinctly muttered "ouch!" drifted back to the little group still seated at the table.

Polly giggled, while Sadie looked concerned. Violet rolled her eyes at the ceiling, and went on eating her suet pudding.

Elizabeth's mind was on the incident at the Tudor Arms. If the three musketeers were doing mischief in the car park, it was very likely that at some time that evening they were actually inside the pub. If so, it was possible that yet another young man had been poisoned. She needed to talk to Earl, and as soon as possible.

She excused herself from the table, thus bringing an end to the pleasant lunch. She was about to leave when Sadie exclaimed, "What happened to the soap? Half of it's missing."

Violet darted a suspicious look at Polly, who

hotly declared, "I ain't got it. I never touched the soap. Honest I didn't."

She looked so upset Elizabeth leaned forward and plucked out one of the remaining packets from the box. "No one's accusing you of anything, Polly. Here you are. You may have this one."

Polly smiled her pleasure. "Thank you, m'm." She took the packet and tucked it into the pocket of her skirt, with a defiant little toss of her head at Violet.

"Martin," Violet muttered. "What on earth does that old fool want with scented soap?"

"More'n likely he wants to smell nice for that lottery lady friend of his," Sadie said with a grin.

"More than likely he wants to *give* her the soap," Violet snapped. "He's given her just about everything else."

"Oo, sounds naughty." Sadie dug Polly in the ribs.

"That's enough, Sadie." Violet waved a hand at the girls. "Get these dishes washed at once. Polly, it's time you went back to your office work."

Both girls took their time getting to their feet. Polly left, presumably to return to the office to finish the rent notices, and Sadie began clearing away the dishes, piling them on the sink ready to wash. Meanwhile, Violet brought the ironing board out from the pantry and set it up in the corner of the kitchen.

Leaving them to their tasks, Elizabeth took the dogs for a short run on the lawn. She found the fresh air and exercise useful in clearing her mind, giving her a chance to concentrate on the problem of what to do about the three musketeers. They had to be apprehended, of course, and made to pay for the damage they had done. More important, if they were responsible for the deaths of those young men, then they belonged in prison, where they could hurt no one else.

She would have to discuss it with Earl. This very evening. Cheered immensely at the thought, she bounded after the dogs.

Polly decided to take the long way back to the office via the back stairs, which would lead her past the east wing. It took several minutes longer to go that way, but there was always the chance she'd bump into Sam, and she took every chance she could get.

To her intense delight, she heard the roar of Jeeps as she dawdled across the courtyard, which signaled the return of the American officers. They must not have had a mission that day, unless they had a night mission and were coming back for a rest before they took off.

Anxiously she waited as the Jeeps drew closer, deathly afraid that Sam wasn't with them. Her leap of joy at the sight of him almost made her cry out, but she knew better than that. Sam got cross with her if she caused a fuss when she saw him. The other men teased him and he didn't like that.

Actually, she rather liked the things they said about her and Sam. Made her feel as though they belonged together, like Greer Garson and Walter Pidgeon. One day Sam would feel the same way about it, too.

She stood back in a doorway until Sam climbed out of his Jeep, then she sauntered across the courtyard as if she'd just that minute arrived. Sam was talking to one of the men with him and didn't seem to notice her. But then she saw his companion nudge his arm and nod his head in her direction.

Sam looked at her then and she waved to him, giving him her widest smile. "How are you, Sam?" she called out.

"Better now that he's seen you," his friend answered. He grinned at Sam. "Guess I'd better leave you two alone."

Sam growled something Polly didn't catch, but the other man hurried off, leaving Sam alone with her in the courtyard.

She advanced toward him, worried by the set look on his face. "I was just passing by," she said, as she reached him. "On me way back to the office. I just had lunch."

He nodded, turning his face away from her so she couldn't see the bad side.

Desperate to get some word out of him she blurted out, "You're back early. I hope you don't have to go up tonight."

"You've gotta stop worrying about me."

She could have cried at the cold words. "I'll never stop worrying about you, Sam. Never."

He faced her then, his face bleak, his eyes so full of misery she thought her heart would break. "Polly, we can't go on like this. It's tough on both of us."

Terrified he was going to cut off her contact with him, she said quickly, "I won't bother you, Sam, honest. All I want is to talk to you now and then. That's all."

"It's not all." He shoved his hands into the pockets of his pants. "You want a lot more and I can't give it to you."

The ache started in her throat again, so bad she could hardly swallow. "Just tell me one thing. Is it because of your face or is it my age?"

He tilted his chin and closed his eyes. "Polly —"

"Cos if it is your face, well, you know I don't care one bit about your scars, and if it's me age, I'm getting older every day. In a year or two you won't even notice the difference. Honest."

He just stood there with a sort of lost puppy look on his face. The ache spread to her heart. "I have to know, Sam. It's not fair to treat me like this when I don't know why."

After a long moment he said quietly, "You're right. It's not. You said something about a movie you wanted to see?"

She nodded eagerly, willing to go anywhere

with him. Anywhere in the world. "*The Philadel-phia Story*. But you said you'd seen it."

"I guess I can see it again. I have a weekend pass. I'll pick you up at your house tomorrow night. Around six-thirty?"

"I'll be waiting!" Wild with excitement she hesitated, wanting desperately to seal their date with a hug. She was disappointed when he gave her a brief nod and hurried off, leaving her no choice but to follow more slowly.

By the time she reached the back door and climbed the stairs, he had disappeared into his quarters. She would just have to wait until to-morrow night now. That was two whole days to get through. How in the world was she going to wait that long?

Hugging herself, she wandered down the great hall, knowing that nothing mattered any-more except the fact that Sam had asked her out again, and that she was going to spend a whole evening with him in North Horsham, cuddling up with him in the back seat of the pictures. It was a dream come true. At last.

When Elizabeth returned to the house with the dogs it was to find the kitchen door securely locked. Wondering why Violet hadn't men-tioned she was going out, Elizabeth made her way around to the front door, the dogs at her heels, hoping that someone was around to let her in.

Martin was probably sound asleep in his

room, and wouldn't hear the bell ring. Polly was in the office, but if she had shut the door she wouldn't hear it either. That left Sadie, who could be anywhere in the depths of the manor too far from the door to hear the bell.

Just as soon as she could afford it, Elizabeth promised herself, she would have an electric bell system installed in the manor, so that anyone anywhere in the house could hear when someone was at the front door. Goodness knows how many visitors they missed because of the old-fashioned bell pull.

It was all very well to want to keep the traditions and trappings of the Manor House the way they had always been, but modern technology certainly had its advantages.

Sighing heavily, Elizabeth tugged on the bell rope. She could barely hear the muffled jangle of the bell on the other side of the solid oak door. Gracie wandered down the steps again, and George chased after her, ignoring Elizabeth's commands to stay.

It took her a few minutes to corral both dogs and urge them back up the steps. The door still hadn't been opened. She waited until her patience gave out, then tugged on the rope again with both hands. Not that it made the bell ring any louder, but it made her feel better.

The dogs looked longingly down the steps, tongues hanging out the sides of their mouths, and she sternly ordered them to stay put. Again she waited. If Martin had heard the bell, it

120

would take him several minutes to climb the stairs to the hallway. She would just have to be patient a few minutes longer.

Marge Gunther puffed and panted as she reached the top of the hill. Time was running out, and she still hadn't got half the things on her list. It didn't look as if she was going to win any prizes.

Throwing caution to the winds, she plunked herself down on the wooden bench that sat close to the railings at the edge of the cliffs. Might as well catch her breath. No sense in killing herself for a packet of lemonade powder and a bottle of lavender water, though the nylons would have been nice.

She was just a few minutes away from the Manor House now. Still time to go up there and ask for donations, and get back to the village in time for tea. Going downhill was faster. In the old days she could run up and down this hill in a matter of minutes. Now she was lucky to make it up here at all.

The view was nice from this spot. Long sandy beaches, completely deserted, the sweep of chalky cliffs around the cove, and little fluffy white caps on the waves. Far out to sea she could see the gray smudge of a ship, and for a moment wished she was on it, on her way to America. They had no bombs in America. Or land mines on the beaches. Not like here. It had been so long since she'd sat on the sand warming herself in the sun. So long since the kids had run back and forth, in and out of the water, carrying their little buckets and spades. How she missed those days.

Lost in her memories, she didn't hear the footsteps until someone stepped in front of her, blocking her view of the ocean. She started up, then sank back when she recognized Nellie Smith.

"I've just been up the Manor House," Nellie said, before Marge could speak. "Look at what I got up there!" She held out her basket, which was a lot fuller than Marge's.

Trying not to show the resentment that gripped her, Marge peered in the basket. That settled it. She didn't have a hope in hell of getting that much by tea time. "What's that?" She pointed to a pretty pastel pink package.

"It's scented soap." Nellie picked it up and held it out to her. "Go on, have a sniff."

Marge sniffed. "Smells lovely."

"It's orange blossom. Really exotic. I got it from the butler. He had it in his pocket. I couldn't believe he was carrying something like this around in his pocket." Nellie took back the packet and held it to her nose. "I know we got soap on the list, but if Rita thinks she's getting her paws on this she's got another think coming. This is mine."

Marge was immediately seized with a burning desire to have a packet of scented soap. "Did he have any more?"

Nellie gave her a sly look. "Perhaps. Anyhow, you won't have much time to go up there and get back to the village in time for tea. You'll be disqualified if you're late."

"I'll make time." Marge surged to her feet and took a firm grip on her basket. A packet of that soap was worth a dozen bottles of lavender water. "I'll see you at Bessie's bake shop."

Nellie looked put out, but Marge was past caring. If Lady Elizabeth's butler was giving out scented soap for free, she was going to get hers. With grim determination, she set out for the Manor House.

Chapter 8

Elizabeth stood impatiently at the front door, still waiting for someone to open it for her. She was about to give up and go down to the back entrance when the sound of bolts being slid back brought a rush of relief. It was a long walk to the other end of the manor, and without their leashes the dogs would have been difficult to control.

Elizabeth knew, from the agonizingly slow movements of the bolts, that it was Martin on the other side of the door. She waited, tapping her foot and making warning noises at the dogs, while the final bolt slid out of its socket, and the door began to open.

Both dogs, no doubt anxious to get at their water bowls, charged the door together. It flew inward, amid a flurry of thumps, yelps, and curses. Wincing, Elizabeth stepped into the hallway.

Martin was flat on his back, one hand grimly holding onto Gracie's tail, while George circled anxiously around the two of them.

Elizabeth leaned over Martin's prone body and asked anxiously, "Are you all right?"

Martin blinked up at her. "Run for your life.

We are being attacked by a herd of hungry wolves."

Relieved that he appeared not to be injured, Elizabeth said mildly, "It's just George and Gracie, Martin. You can let go now."

As if to echo her words, Gracie turned her head until her mouth was an inch or two from the wrinkled hand that held her, and uttered a soft growl of protest.

Martin hastily let go.

Elizabeth helped him to struggle up, while he muttered fiercely to himself. "There you are," she said, when he was finally on his feet. "You're not dizzy, are you?"

"I'm always dizzy these days." He slapped his trousers with his palms then apparently realized whom he was addressing. "I do beg your pardon, madam. I was under the mistaken impression that you were that other woman."

"There's another woman?" Elizabeth looked around. "To whom are you referring, Martin?"

Martin looked confused. "She was here a minute ago. I'd just gone back to my room when I heard the dratted bell again. I thought she'd come back to ask for something else."

"Something else?"

"Yes, madam." He shuffled over to the door and began sliding the bolts back in place. "Something else on that dratted list."

Elizabeth wrinkled her brow. "I think I'd better help you back to your room, Martin. You can lie down for a while and I'm sure you'll feel better."

"I tried lying down." He grunted with the weight of the thick iron latch as he lifted it into its slot. "Every time I lie down someone rings that pesky bell and I have to come all the way back up here."

"Oh, dear," Elizabeth said, feeling guilty. "I'm afraid that was me. I had to go back down the steps after the dogs. You must have opened the door while I was down there."

Martin stared at her. "That was you, madam? I don't understand. You didn't look at all yourself. You looked shorter and . . . ahem . . . younger, if I may be so bold." He shook his head. "And why would you need a list?"

"I don't have a list, Martin."

"Well somebody had a list. That was the reason I gave her the soap."

"Gave who the soap?"

Martin lifted his hands and let them drop. "I'm afraid I don't remember, madam. You say she was you, but I didn't think she was you because she didn't look in the least like you and if I'd known she was you I most certainly wouldn't have given you the soap since you have a whole box of it downstairs."

Without warning, the bell jangled again.

Elizabeth looked at Martin, who stared back at her as if she'd performed a miracle and rang the bell from the outside.

"Who in the world can that be?" he exclaimed.

"I suggest we open the door and find out," Elizabeth prompted gently.

Grumbling under his breath, Martin began sliding the bolts back one by one, while Elizabeth waited with great curiosity to see who had come calling in the middle of the day.

To her surprise, Marge Gunther stood on the doorstep, a large basket hooked over her arm. "Good afternoon," she began, addressing Martin, who was looking most irritated. Then she caught sight of Elizabeth standing behind him. "Oh, good afternoon, your ladyship." She sounded breathless, and her bosom heaved in distress as she held up a sheet of paper. "I'm so sorry to bother you, m'm, but the Housewives League is holding a scavenger hunt, all proceeds go to our servicemen, and I was wondering if by any chance you had anything on this list you could donate."

"Good great heavens, woman!" Martin waved a feeble arm at her. "I've already given you a packet of very expensive soap. Be grateful for what you have and please refrain from annoying us anymore."

Marge looked startled. "T'weren't me what got any soap. Look!" She held up the basket. "That must have been Nellie. I saw her on the way down."

Martin appeared lost for words, and Elizabeth stepped forward. "If you care to wait here a moment," she said, "I have some of the soap in the kitchen. I'll be happy to send a packet up to you."

Marge's face was wreathed in smiles. "Oh, that's very kind of you, m'm, I'm sure."

"Not at all. Martin, have Mrs. Gunther step inside the hallway while I go down to fetch the soap."

"No need, madam." Martin fumbled in his trousers pocket and pulled out a yellow packet. "I just happen to have a tablet of it here." He held it out to Marge, who rather rudely snatched it from his hand.

"Thank you so much, m'm." She dropped it in her basket. "Now I must be off. I have to be back in the village by three, or I'll be disqualified." Without waiting for an answer, she fled down the steps and set off at a run.

"What in heaven's name is a scrounger hunt?" Martin demanded, as he once more began shooting the heavy bolts back in place.

"Not scrounger. It's scavenger." Elizabeth headed for the stairs. "It's like a treasure hunt, I suppose. You have a list of everyday items on it and you have to find as many as you can. Another one of Rita's attempts to bask in glory. Still, it's for a good cause, I suppose." She paused, glancing back at Martin who was still struggling with the bolts. Not only would they have an electrical bell system, she silently vowed, but a modern lock on the door as well. "Thank you for donating the soap, Martin," she called out. "I'll replace it with one from downstairs."

Having heaved the latch back in place, Martin turned to face her. "Thank you, madam. I shall appreciate that. I would like the soap as a gift for a very good friend of mine."

Since Martin hadn't left the house in years, and to the best of Elizabeth's knowledge, had no friends, she had to assume he was referring to Beatrice Carr, the "lottery lady" as Sadie called her.

She was halfway up the stairs when she heard the bell clanging again. It didn't take much brainpower to guess that this was yet another member of the Housewives League. Apparently word had leaked out about the scented soap being given away at the Manor House. Deciding to let Martin handle it in his own inimitable way, Elizabeth resumed climbing the stairs.

As she entered the office, Polly looked up, seeming surprised to see her. "Has he gone already?" she asked, then added somewhat belatedly, "m'm?"

"Has who gone?" Elizabeth drew off her gloves and began removing the pins from her hat.

"Major Monroe, m'm. Didn't Martin tell you? The major was here looking for you. I sent him to wait in the library 'cause I knew you wouldn't be long."

Elizabeth's hand paused in midair. "Major Monroe?"

"Yes, m'm." Polly glanced at the clock on the wall. "He's been there for about twenty minutes or so."

Elizabeth made an enormous effort to sound indifferent. "Oh, dear. I wonder what he wants. I suppose I'd better go down and find out."

"Yes, m'm. I'd certainly do that if I were you." Polly grinned at her.

Good great heavens, Elizabeth thought in despair. Did everyone in the household know how she felt about the man? If she was that transparent, did Earl have any inkling of her feelings for him? The thought that he might indeed be aware of them had her so agitated she dropped the hat pins on the floor.

"I'll get those, m'm." Polly darted out from behind her desk. "We don't want to keep the major waiting any longer, now, do we."

Elizabeth eyed her with suspicion. "You seem in a particularly good mood, Polly. Has something happened?"

Polly crouched down to retrieve the pins while Elizabeth removed her hat. "Yes, m'm. I suppose you could say something has." She straightened, her cheeks flushed with excitement. "I'm going to the pictures with Sam tomorrow night."

Elizabeth exclaimed in delight. "Polly, I'm so happy for you. I know how miserable you've been, wondering if he was ever going to ask you out again. This *is* good news."

"Yes, m'm." Polly handed her the pins and returned to her desk. "I'm really, really excited."

"Well, I know you will both have a wonderful time." Elizabeth laid her hat on her desk and patted her hair in place. "How are the rent notices coming?"

"Almost finished." Polly pointed to the thin stack. "That's all that's left."

"Well, I'll come back later to help with them."

"Don't bother, m'm." Polly grinned happily. "Just you go and have a good time with the major."

Elizabeth felt her own cheeks grow warm. It was rather impertinent of the child to say such a thing, but she meant well. "Thank you, Polly. I'll do my best." Her heart thumping in anticipation, she hurried from the office.

Earl had his back to her when she entered the library. She was immediately reminded of the first day she'd seen him. He had stood much the same, feet apart, hands behind his back, shoulders squared, his gaze intent on her father's collection of classic literature.

For a moment she stood, drinking in the sight of him. These memories were all she'd have left when he returned to America, and she wanted to imprint each one on her mind, so they would stay with her forever.

"It would be nice to have the time to read all of these books," he said, as he turned to greet her.

131

She smiled. "I read most of them as a child, but I'm afraid I don't read too many books these days. Mostly newspapers, magazines, something that doesn't take a lot of my attention at one time."

He nodded, watching her with a grave expression that unsettled her. She could never tell what he was thinking when he looked at her like that. Sometimes she thought it was better she didn't know.

"How are you?" She glanced at the grandfather clock in the corner of the room. "You're back early today."

"I have to leave again after dinner."

"Oh." She knew what that meant. He had a night mission. Her stomach seemed to turn inside out at the thought. Determined not to let the fear overwhelm her, she said brightly, "Would you be free to join me for a meal this evening?"

His smile went a long way toward warming the cold place inside her. "Isn't this a little short notice?"

"I'm sure Violet can rustle up something. You've been very generous with supplies from the base. It's high time we returned the favor."

"Well, thanks, but I guess I'll have to take a rain check. I have to be back at the base by six. Maybe tomorrow night?"

"I'll look forward to it." She beckoned to a chair. "I'm glad you're here. I have some things I want to discuss with you."

His eyes sparked with interest. "You've found out who poisoned our guys?"

"Well, not exactly." She sat down, allowing him to do the same. "I visited the Adelaides' farm, and they do have daphne growing in their yard, but that really doesn't prove anything. Though I did notice there were no berries on the bushes."

His eyebrows raised. "That sounds promising."

"There's something else." She told him about the three musketeers, and their escapades at the Tudor Arms.

"They appear to have a grudge against the American airmen, though I'm not sure they'd go as far as poisoning them. Their assaults seem more mischief than anything else. Things like cutting up tires and scribbling messages on walls. Have you heard of anyone else becoming ill?"

Earl shook his head. "Not in the last few days, no. That doesn't mean these guys are not responsible. Maybe they didn't realize the berries were poisonous. They could have just wanted to give our guys the runs."

"According to Desmond, the berries are extremely bitter and quite caustic. I can't imagine any of them actually eating them."

"Unless they thought eating them would make them irresistible to women or something."

Elizabeth raised her eyebrows.

Earl shrugged. "You'd be surprised what

these guys will do when they're desperate. They'll believe anything."

"It's possible, I suppose. Though I'm more inclined to think the berries were added to something the victims might have eaten or drunk and they were unaware of their presence. Something such as stout or bitter ale, for instance. As Desmond said, if the men drank enough alcohol, they wouldn't notice the odd taste."

"That could be, too."

"The question is, how do we prove it?"

Earl stretched his legs out in front of him, eased himself back in the chair and frowned in concentration. He looked so comfortable and at ease, it warmed Elizabeth's heart just to look at him. "I guess," he said at last, "that we could use a decoy."

It took her a moment to realize what he meant. "A decoy? Isn't that rather dangerous?"

"It depends on who's the decoy and how the situation is handled." He wrestled with his thoughts for a moment or two. "It would have to be someone with red hair. Someone who knows how to take care of himself."

Elizabeth waited, unashamedly gazing at his face, while he pursued the problem.

Finally, he snapped his fingers. "Got it! Joe Hanson. He's just the guy. He's a boxer, and a good one."

Elizabeth leaned forward eagerly. "And he has red hair?"

Earl smiled. "Red as a Wyoming sunset."

"But will he do it?"

"I think so. He knew two of the guys who died and was pretty cut up about it. I think he'll welcome the chance to get the jerks who did this."

"It could mean trouble for him."

"Not if he's careful. The trick will be getting these jokers to try it again. Always supposing they haven't been scared off by the deaths." Earl's expression turned wary. "Joe might have a better chance of that if he had one of the local girls playing up to him. If that's what's bugging them it might stir them up enough to give it another shot."

Elizabeth gave him a sharp look. "I don't think I'd want any of our young girls involved. I would never forgive myself if one of them were hurt."

"It's not the girls our man is after. It's the GIs. Besides, Joe's a good man. I'd trust him to handle it."

Doubtfully, Elizabeth considered the proposition. "Well, if I were to suggest someone, and I'm not saying I am at this point, I'd say that Sadie seems like a young woman who can take good care of herself. I think she would be happy to contribute."

"Well, why don't we ask them?" Earl got to his feet. "I'll go find Joe and you can ask Sadie how she feels about it. I'll meet you back here in about half an hour, and I'll bring Joe with me."

Reluctantly, Elizabeth stood, still uncertain

about this whole project. "I'll have a word with Sadie, but if she shows the slightest hesitation, I'll forget the whole idea."

"Agreed." He crossed to the door and opened it for her. As she passed through the doorway he laid a hand on her shoulder. "Don't worry, Elizabeth. I wouldn't set Sadie up with anyone I couldn't trust."

She smiled at that. "Knowing my housemaid, Major Monroe, I'd say that it's your young man you should be worrying about." To her delight, she could hear him chuckling as he strode away from her down the great hall.

The hallway was deserted when she hurried down the stairs. Martin must have dealt with whoever had rung the doorbell. She hoped he wasn't giving out too much of the soap. She was rather looking forward to using some of it herself.

The kitchen was also empty when she peered inside, but she could see the housemaid's stout figure through the window. She was in the garden pegging the laundry on the line. Elizabeth quickly crossed the kitchen and went out through the back door.

Sadie looked worried as Elizabeth approached. "What is it, m'm?" she asked, her arms holding a damp sheet to her chest. "Am I doing something wrong?"

"Not at all, Sadie." Elizabeth viewed the four long lines of laundry flapping in the breeze.

"Everything looks marvelous. It will all dry quite soon in this wind."

"Yes, m'm." Sadie fished a wooden peg out of her apron pocket and hooked a corner of the sheet over the line. "As long as it doesn't rain, that is. That's why Violet said to get it all out this afternoon."

"I'd like a word with you when you're finished." Elizabeth looked at the basket, which appeared to have one remaining sheet in it. "I'll wait for you in the kitchen."

"Very well, m'm. I'll be there in a tick."

Elizabeth headed back to the kitchen, still uneasy about the task she was about to set for Sadie. It was one thing to ask for help in apprehending what could be dangerous criminals, but to put a young woman into harm's way was something else indeed. If it was anyone other than Sadie, she wouldn't have even considered it.

On the other hand, as Earl had pointed out, the target of the poisonings had been confined to Americans with red hair. Since Sadie was neither American, nor a redhead, it seemed unlikely she would be singled out.

Elizabeth sat down at the kitchen table and rested her chin on her hands. She would simply present her case to Sadie, and watch the girl's reaction. If she showed the slightest bit of concern, then she and Earl would have to come up with a different plan. She could only hope that it didn't turn out badly for either her housemaid, or the young man Earl had picked for the task.

★ ★ ★

The babble in Bessie's bake shop rose to a crescendo as the remaining members of the Housewives League straggled through the door.

Rita stared hard at the clock on the mantle-piece above the brick fireplace, determined to cut off the competition the second the big hand reached one.

The last person through the door was Marge Gunther. She came hurtling into the tearoom, basket bouncing on her arm, her face as red as a beetroot.

Rita stared pointedly at her, then back at the clock. The big hand barely touched the first figure of the one. "You're lucky," she pronounced, as Marge panted up to her. "One second more and you would have been disqualified."

Too breathless to speak, Marge nodded her thanks and collapsed on a chair at the nearest table.

Rita cast a disparaging eye around the tearoom. Everyone had returned with their baskets. Now all that remained was to count up everyone's items. Then they could all enjoy some of Bessie's delicious sandwiches and cakes.

Having looked forward to this moment ever since the idea of the scavenger hunt had first been conceived, Rita clapped her hands together. "Ladies!"

As usual, everyone ignored her. Deploring the

need to raise her voice like a fishwife, Rita took a deep breath and bellowed, "Will you bloody pay attention, please!"

Unfortunately, for some mysterious reason, everyone stopped talking just as she yelled, thus provoking some thoroughly disgusted glances from other customers in the tearoom.

Rita clamped her lips together, inwardly fuming. To make matters worse, Nellie Smith giggled, bringing smiles to several of the housewives sitting close to her. Rita dealt with the unfortunate girl with one of her drop-dead glares.

She could tell, by the pile of odds and sods in Nellie's basket, that she would probably win the prize, and the thought irked her to no end. There didn't seem a lot she could do about it, so she would just have to grin and bear it. And come up with something else that Nellie couldn't win. Like a knitting contest or something. Nellie couldn't tie her shoelaces without help.

"Did you get some soap?" Nellie asked Marge, who finally seemed to have recovered her breath.

Marge nodded in triumph. She reached inside her basket and fished out a yellow packet, which she waved in the air. "Scented soap," she declared. "It smells bloomin' smashing."

"Oo, let me smell!" There was a horrible scraping sound of chairs being pushed back as the ladies eagerly crowded around Marge.

"I was the one that told her about it," Nellie loudly complained. "Look, I got some, too!"

"Where did you get it?" Maisie Parsons demanded. "I never saw nothing like that. My granddaughter would love some of that."

"You'll have to go up to the Manor House to get it then," Marge told her. "Lady Elizabeth's barmy butler gave it to me."

"He gave me some, too!" Nellie shouted, obviously put out by having been robbed of all the attention.

No one paid her any notice.

Rita decided it was time to take back the floor. She clapped her hands again and, taking care not to raise her voice too high this time, declared, "Everyone who has bootlaces in their basket, hold up your hand."

"Does he have any of that soap left?" Maisie asked, quite rudely ignoring Rita's attempts to shush her up.

Marge shrugged. "Dunno. He pulled it out of his trousers pocket. He might have more in there. I couldn't tell."

"I'm surprised Nellie didn't take it all off him," Clara Rigglesby said, with a sour look on her face.

Nellie looked offended. "What, go in his trousers pockets? What d'you blinking take me for?"

"You've been in just about everyone else's trousers," Clara snapped.

Everyone laughed at that, even the other customers.

Nellie looked as if she might take a swipe at Clara's face, but Rita hurriedly intervened.

"I think that's enough," she said loudly. "Now, will you please hold up your hands if you have bootlaces."

"I'll go up to the Manor House this evening," Maisie said, peering into Marge's basket. "If that butler has any of that smelly soap left I'm going to get some and send it to my grand-daughter in London."

"You can't," Nellie said, sounding peevish. "The scavenger hunt is over."

"Don't mean I can't go ask for some." Maisie squinted maliciously at Nellie. "Don't tell me you're going to give that soap to the servicemen. They start smelling all pretty and flowery when they're in the trenches and the rest of 'em will think they're poofs."

"Never mind what I'm going to do with the soap." Nellie glared back at her. "You can't go up to the Manor House and just ask for it. That's begging."

"Not if she takes some of her gingerbread up there," Marge said slyly. "I bet that butler would love to swap some of his soap for Maisie's gin-gerbread. He looks like a good meal would do him good."

"Good idea," Maisie said, smiling happily at her friend. "I just baked a batch this morning. I'll take some up there in exchange for the soap."

"Bootlaces!" Rita howled, abandoning all restraint. "We'll be here all afternoon if you don't start holding up your hands. Now who's got bootlaces?"

Eyes blazing, Nellie turned on her. "Oh, tie your bloody bootlaces around your neck and strangle yourself."

That did it. Trembling with outrage, Rita pointed a shaky finger at her. "You're disqualified, Nellie Smith. For disrupting the proceedings. What's more, you're suspended from the Housewives League for a month."

Amid gasps of horror, Nellie got up from the table, picked up her basket and said with a malicious sneer, "All right. If I'm disqualified then I'm taking all this stuff with me. Except these." She took out a packet of bootlaces and flung them at Rita. "And you know what you can do with those."

With that she turned and headed for the door. By the time Rita had thought of a suitable retort, Nellie had disappeared into the street.

Chapter 9

Elizabeth was becoming impatient by the time Sadie came bustling back into the kitchen, a worried frown on her face.

"You're not going to sack me, are you, m'm? I don't know what I'd do if I didn't have this job. I mean, this is my home now, and I'd have to start all over again and —"

"Sadie," Elizabeth said gently. "I'm not going to let you go. You are far too valuable to this household."

"Oh, whew!" Sadie flopped down on a chair, fanning her face with her hand. Then, apparently realizing she hadn't been invited to do so, jumped up to her feet again. "Beg your pardon, m'm. I didn't mean to take liberties. I was just so relieved to hear you weren't going to sack me. I'm ever so happy here, and I wouldn't want to have to leave."

"Sit down, Sadie." Elizabeth smiled at her. "I just wanted to ask you a favor, that's all. But before I do, I want you to promise me that if you feel you'd rather not accept my proposal, I shall quite understand, and your decision shall in no way compromise your position in this household. I hope I make myself clear?"

Sadie looked even more worried now. "Oo, 'eck, it sounds serious."

"Well, it is, rather." Elizabeth sighed. "Sadie, I must ask for your solemn promise that you will not repeat a word of what I say to you now, and that you will tell no one about the favor I'm about to ask you. It's extremely important that no one knows what you are doing. If word got out it would not only jeopardize our plan, it could very well land you in a great deal of trouble."

"Blimey." Sadie's face paled. "Has it got anything to do with the war effort? 'Cos if so, I'll do anything you ask. I'd love to get one back at those buggers what bombed me out of me house."

Elizabeth cleared her throat. "Well, no, not exactly. It's to do with the American airmen who died recently. I'm sure you must have heard about it."

"Oh, yeah!" Sadie nodded her head. "Some kind of illness going around, so they say. I only hope to Gawd we don't get it here."

"Yes, well, I think that's very unlikely." Elizabeth paused, then added carefully, "It's quite possible that the men who died were poisoned."

Sadie's eyes widened. "On purpose?"

"We think so. Mostly because all the men who died were American airmen, and they all had red hair."

Sadie's look of amazement was almost comical. "Red hair? Someone poisoned them because they had red hair?"

144

"We think so, yes."

"But why the heck . . . ?"

"We don't know. Which brings me to the point." Elizabeth drew in a deep breath. "Major Monroe and I suspect that whoever gave those men the poison might very well do so again. We think it was given to the men while they were at the Tudor Arms. Major Monroe is suggesting that we use a decoy in the hopes of inducing the men to attempt to poison him, thereby catching them red-handed, so to speak."

"I see." Sadie chewed her bottom lip. "Seems like a good idea. Though a bit dodgy. What do I have to do?"

"Well, the major thought his decoy might hasten matters if he was . . . ah . . . showing a good deal of interest in a local girl, which could well be an incentive for the actions of these criminals."

Sadie's eyes gleamed. "You mean I'm supposed to neck with him?"

Elizabeth swallowed. "I believe that's the popular term, yes."

"In public?"

Elizabeth hid her smile. Sadie's look of outrage was just a little hypocritical. "Well, within the boundaries of good taste, of course."

"Of course." She paused, her eyes narrowing. "What's he look like? I don't think I could neck with just anyone. Even if it is for a good cause."

"I'm afraid I don't know. I haven't met him. But Major Monroe is bringing him to the library . . ." Elizabeth glanced at the clock, "in about ten minutes. If you think this is something you can do, I suggest we join them and discuss the matter. Major Monroe assures me the young man is very capable and you'll be quite safe in his hands."

Sadie sniffed. "Begging your pardon, m'm, but I haven't met a man yet who can say that."

"I didn't mean it in that way." Thoroughly uncomfortable, Elizabeth sought for the right words. She was decidedly out of her depth and already regretting she'd ever agreed to this plan. "What I meant —"

"It's all right, m'm. Really. I was just being sarky." Sadie pushed her chair back and stood. "If it means catching a bunch of murdering bleeders, I'll be happy to do whatever it takes. I know a lot of people don't like the Yanks, but that's because they don't know them. It don't give them no right to go around killing them, that's for sure."

"I heartily agree." Elizabeth rose, anticipation already tingling at the prospect of seeing Earl again. "Then let us talk to the men, and find out what we can do to rectify this unfortunate situation."

Sadie obediently followed her up to the library, where Earl was already waiting for them. A burly young man stood next to him, and he snatched off his cap the minute the women entered the room.

Earl had been right about his hair, Elizabeth

thought, gazing at the cropped copper thatch on the young man's head. He definitely had red hair. She glanced at her housemaid, who seemed to have acquired a bashfulness totally unlike her usual demeanor.

Eyes cast down, hands clasped in front of her, Sadie displayed the perfect picture of a shy maiden about to meet a possible suitor.

Earl, who was acquainted with Sadie's forthright manner, seemed amused. "Your ladyship, Sadie, I'd like you both to meet second lieutenant, Joseph Hanson. Joe, this is Lady Elizabeth Hartleigh Compton, the lady of the manor, and Miss Sadie Buttons, an important member of Lady Elizabeth's household."

The young man inclined his head in Elizabeth's direction, then nodded at Sadie, his expression lacking emotion in typical military indifference. "Pleasure to meet you, ma'am. You, too, ma'am."

"The pleasure's entirely mine," Sadie said demurely.

Wondering how long her housemaid would be able to keep up the charade, Elizabeth said briskly, "It's a pleasure to meet you, Lieutenant. I understand you're willing to help us apprehend some rather beastly hooligans."

"Yes, ma'am."

Elizabeth drew Sadie forward. "Sadie has very kindly offered to assist us in this endeavor." She glanced at Earl. "Do you have any specific instructions for her?"

"I've explained it all to Joe," Earl said, putting a hand on the young man's shoulder. "You need to make it look as if you're on a date at the pub, keep your eyes open and report back to me if you see anything suspicious. That's all, really." He smiled at Sadie. "Just pretend he's your boyfriend for the evening, all right?"

"Sounds good to me." Sadie's eyes gleamed, giving Elizabeth the impression that she rather liked the looks of her impending escort.

The young's man cheeks turned a pale shade of pink. There was no doubt as to who was going to get the most out of this situation, Elizabeth thought. She could only hope that Sadie behaved herself and didn't do anything to embarrass the charming lieutenant.

"You will be careful?" Elizabeth said, appealing to Lieutenant Hanson. "Four men have already died. I should hate to have another on my conscience."

"Don't worry, ma'am. I'll be careful."

"And you will take care of Sadie?"

"Yes, ma'am. She'll be safe with me."

Sadie's expression mirrored skepticism at that remark, and Elizabeth hastily turned to Earl. "I suppose it will be all right, then. When should they do this?"

"It will have to be tomorrow night." Earl peered at his watch. "We should be back by then."

So her hunch had been right, Elizabeth thought miserably. They were going on a mission this evening. "Very well," she said brightly. She looked at the lieutenant. "I'll leave it up to you two to make the arrangements."

"Yes, ma'am. Thank you, ma'am. Sir?" He saluted Earl, who returned it.

"Thank you, Joe. Perhaps Sadie can show you around the grounds before you leave, and you can get better acquainted." He glanced at Elizabeth. "Is that all right?"

She nodded. "Quite all right."

Sadie abandoned her pretense of shy maiden. "Come on, luv." She grabbed the startled young man by the arm. "I'll show you the sights."

Looking a little as if he were being led to slaughter, Joe followed her from the room. The door closed behind them, leaving Elizabeth staring after them with a sense of uneasiness.

"They will be all right, won't they?" she murmured.

"I think they're gonna be just fine." Earl moved closer to her, and placed his hands on her shoulders. "Try not to worry, Elizabeth. I wouldn't have suggested this if I'd considered it too dangerous. I've warned Joe not to take his eyes off their drinks, and not to eat anything while they are at the pub."

Elizabeth let out her breath in a sigh. "That sounds all right. But I won't feel comfortable about them until they are both safely back from their mission." She looked up at him, unsettled by his nearness to her. She could smell a faint aroma of an unfamiliar fragrance. It was both refreshing and disturbing, like the man who wore it. "That goes for you, too."

His eyebrows rose. "Me?"

"Tonight, I mean."

"Ah. Well, try not to worry about me either."

"You might as well tell me not to breathe."

His eyes darkened, and her heart skipped a beat. "I like the idea of you worrying about me," he said softly.

She only had to tilt her chin, lean in a little closer, and she had no doubt what the outcome would be. She wanted that kiss, longed for it, ached for it, and for a second or two contemplated abandoning her principles and going for it.

Years of conditioning, however, could not be denied. She was the daughter of an earl and he was a married man. Being a divorced woman was a disgrace enough already. She could not compound her mistakes.

"I worry about all of you." She drew back, forcing him to drop his hands. "You and your men have become a second family to us all here, and we all worry about you."

If he was disappointed by her withdrawal, he showed no sign of it. Instead, he reached for his cap, saying lightly, "I have to get back to the base. Is our date for tomorrow night still on?"

She looked at him in surprise. Surely he didn't expect her to accompany him to the pub as well?

"Our dinner," he reminded her. "You invited me, didn't you?"

"Oh, of course! I'm so sorry, I forgot. This business with Sadie and your lieutenant put it completely out of my mind."

He sighed. "Forgotten so soon. I guess I over-estimated my importance."

He'd made it sound as if he were teasing, but she sensed there was genuine disappointment behind his words. If he only knew how much she longed to forget who she was, who he was. Who knew how much more time they might have together? Would it really be so wrong to snatch what little happiness they could in these dreadful days of uncertainty and peril?

She'd had these moments before, when her hopeless love for him had almost outweighed her common sense. She'd overcome the temptations then as she had done so a moment ago, but how long . . . oh, how long could she go on denying herself what she wanted so desperately?

She stepped toward him, bringing them closer once more. "I hope you know," she said unsteadily, "that you are intensely important to me. In every way."

The sad expression in his eyes broke her heart. "I know that you're a strong woman, Elizabeth, with values and morals far beyond anyone I've ever met before. I admire you for that, yet at the same time, I wish it could be different."

Her voice trembled as she answered him. "So do I, Earl. Oh, so do I."

He gave her a wry smile that was more shattering than anything he could have said. "I look forward to our dinner tomorrow night." He reached for her hand and held it in his warm grasp.

"Take good care of yourself," she murmured.

"I'll be back. That's a promise." He squeezed her hand gently and let her go.

Before she could say anymore, he was gone.

Martin seemed particularly agitated that evening when he arrived for supper. Violet had managed to find fish roes, and was serving them on toast with fried tomatoes and mushrooms, accompanied by thick crusty bread and margarine.

The delicious smell of the fried food had wafted up to the library, where Elizabeth and Polly were finishing off the rent notices. Elizabeth could tell that Polly was anxious to go home, no doubt having her appetite stimulated by the smell of fried fish, and it was a relief to get the final rent notice in its envelope ready to put in the post the next morning.

Martin was already in the kitchen when Elizabeth entered, hovering around the kitchen table as if searching for something.

Violet stood at the stove, flipping fish roes around in a large frying pan. Sadie hadn't arrived, as yet. Elizabeth was rather anxious to find out how things had gone between her and Lieutenant Hanson.

She sat down at the table and looked at Martin, who was still fidgeting around. "Are you looking for something?" she asked at last.

Martin looked flustered. "I beg your pardon, madam. I was just wondering if you had any of that scented soap left."

Elizabeth scanned the table, but the box of soap seemed to have disappeared. "Well, I did, but I don't know what happened to it."

"I put it in the pantry," Violet said, still with her back to them. A loud sizzling accompanied her words as she dropped two halves of a tomato into the pan. "Out of harm's way, so to speak."

Martin slowly twisted around until he faced her. "If you are inferring that I might steal the soap, I'd like to inform you that madam offered to replace the packages of soap I gave away today."

"He's right, Violet," Elizabeth said, smiling at Martin. "He gave out two packages of soap and I promised I'd replace them."

"Three," Martin said, holding up three fingers.

Elizabeth looked at him in surprise. "Three?"

"Yes, madam. Just a little while ago. Another lady came to the door asking for soap."

Elizabeth frowned. "But I thought the scavenger hunt was over this afternoon. Didn't Marjorie Gunther say she would be disqualified if she didn't get back to the tearoom right away. That was about half past two, surely?"

"Yes, madam. But this lady wasn't collecting for the scrounger hunt."

"Scavenger, Martin."

"Yes, madam."

"Then why did she want the soap?"

"She said it was for her granddaughter. She's living in London, I believe. The granddaughter, not the grandmother. Sadie was in the hallway talking rather loudly to one of those American soldiers at the time, so I couldn't hear everything she said."

Violet clicked her tongue in disgust. "What do they think we are? A blinking charity house? Got a blinking nerve, if you ask me. Coming up here begging for free stuff."

Elizabeth was inclined to agree. "Martin, I think we should tell anyone else who might ask for soap that we have no more. Otherwise we could have the entire village lining up at the door."

"Yes, madam." He began shuffling over to the pantry. "I only gave it to Mrs. Parsons because she said she was so lonely without her granddaughter."

"Parsons?" Elizabeth frowned. "Do I know her?"

"She's one of Rita's Housewives League members," Violet said, sliding the fried tomatoes onto a plate. "Maisie Parsons. She's the one who makes the gingerbread. Won't tell us how

154

she does it, though. Keeps that a secret. As if I care."

Martin, who was almost at the pantry door, paused. "She gave me some of it," he said.

Violet gave him a scathing glance. "Gave you what?"

"Some of her gingerbread." He resumed shuffling. "I'd give you some, but since you don't care for it, I'll keep it for myself." Then he seemed to remember his manners. He turned so swiftly, he almost lost his balance, and had to clutch the doorjamb to remain on his feet. "I'll be happy to share it with you though, madam."

Elizabeth smiled. "Thank you, Martin, but I really don't care for gingerbread. I do appreciate the offer, however."

"Yes, well, you probably wouldn't like it." Once more he turned himself around and disappeared into the pantry.

Violet finished serving up the food and placed the plates on the kitchen table. "Gone to get his soap," she muttered. "Couldn't wait until after supper."

Elizabeth sat down at the table and eyed the fish roes without much enthusiasm. Her concern over Earl, and Sadie's risky appointment tomorrow had robbed her of her appetite.

She picked up her knife and fork, just as Martin wandered out of the pantry carrying three packets of soap.

Violet watched his painfully slow progress across the kitchen with a baleful eye. "I hope you didn't eat too much of that gingerbread and spoil your supper."

Martin gave her a disparaging glare. "I have not touched it. Mrs. Parsons wasn't too complimentary about her cooking, so I was in no great hurry to taste it."

Both Violet and Elizabeth stared at him in surprise.

"Maisie Parsons put down her own cooking?" Violet said, her eyebrows twitching up and down. "I don't believe it. She's proud of that gingerbread. Practically everyone in the village says how good Maisie's gingerbread is."

Martin shuffled over to the table. "May I have your permission to sit down, madam?"

Elizabeth beckoned at his chair. "Of course, Martin. Do sit."

"Thank you, madam."

Violet stood over him while he gradually lowered himself onto his seat. "I want to know what Maisie Parsons said about her gingerbread," she said, arms crossed, her head tilted to one side like an agitated sparrow.

Martin's descent ended in a rush as he dropped the last few inches. He shot a resentful look at Violet. "She said that her gingerbread was moldy and should be disposed of as soon as possible. Or words to that effect."

Violet shook her head and turned back to the stove. "Barmy. Blinking barmy, that's what he is."

Elizabeth wasn't paying her much attention.

She was too busy thinking about Earl, and praying that he would return safely that night. Her world would be shattered all too soon by his inevitable departure. She could only hope it wouldn't be just yet.

She slept fitfully that night, her ears trained for the sound of the returning Jeeps. When she awoke to a gray dawn, her first thoughts were of Earl, and if he had returned safely.

There didn't seem to be any way to find out without sounding overly concerned about his well-being, and she had to content herself with the notion that had anything dreadful happened to him, she would surely have heard by now.

Breakfast started out as rather a quiet affair. Martin was in one of his silent moods, and Violet seemed preoccupied with making a shopping list, a task that had become increasingly daunting since the onset of rationing.

Elizabeth toyed with her oatmeal, until it dawned on her that she had not yet informed Violet that she had invited Earl to dinner. Perhaps she had been afraid of tempting fate. Even now, she was reluctant to mention it, in the event that she had to cancel it for a reason she didn't want to think about.

Engrossed in her gloomy thoughts, she was startled when Sadie burst into the kitchen, singing at the top of her voice.

Martin immediately rose from the table,

struggled over to the sink with his plate, cup and saucer, and placed them on the draining board. "I shall withdraw to attend to my duties, madam," he said, with a cold look at Sadie, who had plopped down at the table next to Violet with a cheery smile. "The kitchen is becoming entirely too crowded."

"Good morning, Marty, me old codswaller," Sadie sang out. "How's your mother off for dripping, then?"

Martin sniffed. "I'll thank you not to use that disgusting cockney vernacular in the presence of her ladyship."

Sadie shot a wary look at Elizabeth as Martin departed at his usual snail's pace. "Sorry, m'm. Didn't mean no disrespect."

"Quite all right, Sadie," Elizabeth murmured. She was engrossed at the moment, trying to think of a way to ask Sadie if she knew if their American guests had returned — one in particular — without arousing unwanted speculation from her staff.

"No, it's not all right," Violet said crossly. "How many times do I have to tell you, Sadie, to speak properly while you are in this house."

"I am speaking properly. Ere, guess who I saw the other day." She nudged Violet's shoulder with her elbow, earning a scathing glance from the housekeeper.

"I haven't the slightest idea, but if you poke me again like that you won't be seeing anyone else for quite a while."

Apparently unimpressed by this threat, Sadie grinned. "Winston Churchill, that's who."

Violet looked up. "Winston Churchill? Where?"

"On the cliffs, that's where. Walking along, he was, just minding his own business."

"You saw our prime minister walking along the cliffs in Sitting Marsh," Violet repeated in disbelief.

"Yes, I did." Sadie nodded emphatically at Elizabeth, who was following the conversation without really taking it in. "I said hello to him."

"And he answered?"

"Not exactly. He sort of touched the brim of his bowler and nodded, then went on walking."

Violet stared at her for a moment longer and then said firmly, "That imagination of yours will get you into trouble one day, my girl. You mark my words."

"I didn't imagine it. I really saw him." Sadie's voice rose in indignation. "Why won't anyone believe me?" She appealed to Elizabeth. "You believe me, m'm, don't you?"

Elizabeth made an effort to concentrate. "The prime minister? I doubt if he'd visit Sitting Marsh without a great deal of pomp and cere-mony. He's a very important man."

Sadie's face registered frustration. "But —"

"That's enough, Sadie!" Violet pounded the table with her fist, making Elizabeth jump. "Enough of your nonsense. Surely you can find something more important to do than torment us with your wild stories? There's oatmeal on the stove. Dish up a plate for yourself and eat your breakfast. It's getting late and you have work to do."

Sadie leaned over her shoulder. "Want me to make a fresh pot of tea, luv?"

The housekeeper pressed her pencil so hard on the sheet of paper in front of her the lead snapped. "I don't know what the world is coming to. It's all the fault of these Americans, that's what it is. Teaching our young girls to disrespect their elders."

Elizabeth bit her tongue. She was not about to get in an argument with her housekeeper in front of Sadie.

"All right, Violet, then." Sadie got up from the table and grabbed a large copper kettle and began filling it with water. "It's just that I'm in a good mood, that's all. The boys all came back safely last night. Or I should say early this morning." She carried the kettle over to the stove, and gave Elizabeth a sly look on the way. "Including the major. I saw them come in."

Elizabeth let out the breath she hadn't known she was holding. He was safe. Once more she could look forward to seeing him. She'd been given another reprieve.

Chapter 10

Violet snapped her head up. "What were you doing up in the middle of the night, Sadie Buttons?"

"I couldn't sleep, could I." Sadie lit the gas jet under the kettle. "I opened me window for a breath of fresh air and saw the Yanks walking in from the courtyard."

Elizabeth seized the opportunity. "Oh, Violet, speaking of the major, I've invited him to supper tonight. I hope that won't present a problem?"

Violet wore a disapproving frown when she muttered, "No, of course not. I've still got some coupons left. I'll see what the butcher's got."

Much as Violet liked Earl, Elizabeth was well aware that her housekeeper found it impossible to condone his relationship with her employer, largely due to her concern that Elizabeth would get her heart broken again. Once was enough in Violet's considered opinion.

In hers, too, Elizabeth thought, but that didn't seem to dampen her feelings for Earl. "I thought you might bake a steak and kidney pie," she suggested. "That shouldn't take up too many coupons and you make such delicious pastry."

Sadie swung around. "Begging your pardon, m'm, but not many of the Yanks like kidney. Alfie had to throw all his pies out because none of the Yanks would touch 'em."

"Oh." Elizabeth exchanged glances with Violet. "Well, in that case, perhaps steak and mushroom?"

To her great relief, Violet nodded. "Just leave it to me," she said. "I'll find something the major will like."

Filled with elation now that her immediate worry was over, Elizabeth rose to her feet. "I shall be in the office this morning if anyone needs me." She looked meaningfully at Sadie, who had been watching her out of the corner of her eye. "I'd like a word with you before you leave this evening."

"Yes, m'm." Sadie stuck her thumb up in the air in a gesture that had to be purely American.

Violet shuddered, but mercifully refrained from commenting as Elizabeth left the room.

When she arrived in the office a few minutes later, Polly was at her desk, sorting out the morning post.

"Got lots of bills in, m'm," she said, when Elizabeth greeted her. "Hope we've got enough money to pay 'em."

"Yes, well, we'll have to decide which are the most important and pay what we can." Elizabeth sat down at her own desk and sighed. Bills. Just as soon as she got them paid, more came in. It was a never-ending battle.

"They was here again last night," Polly said, slitting open yet another long brown envelope.

Elizabeth blinked. She thought at first the girl might be talking about the scavenger hunters. Though the hunt was presumably over yesterday afternoon. Unless it was more people looking for soap. Giving up, she asked, "Who was here last night?"

Polly looked up, her lips pursed and her eyebrows drawn together in an expression Elizabeth couldn't identify. "Them three musketeers," she said, in a hushed tone that was obviously meant to convey deep mystery and explained her odd expression, no doubt gleaned from one of her favorite films. Polly was continually mimicking famous film stars.

Elizabeth, however, was too concerned to be amused. In fact, she felt a distinct chill. "Did you happen to see them again?"

"No, m'm, I didn't. But I stopped by Marlene's hairdresser's this morning to drop off her lunch and they was all talking about it. Marlene said that someone put boards with nails sticking out of them down on the coast road to burst the tires on a Jeep. Then, when it stopped, they beat up the two Yanks inside and left three Ms scribbled on the Jeep."

Elizabeth clenched her fists. It infuriated her that these savages from London were causing

163

trouble in her village. Something had to be done about them.

"Did your sister say who told her about this attack? Did the Americans describe the thugs?"

"I don't know, m'm. Marlene never said." Polly frowned. "I don't know what's wrong with our Marl lately. She don't talk to me the way she used to. She's keeping secrets. She never used to do that."

Elizabeth, her mind on this latest news, muttered absently, "Perhaps she has a new boyfriend."

"Nah, she'd tell me if that was it." Polly sounded worried. "Something's wrong, I just know it. Something she's afraid to tell Ma or even me."

"Well, I'm sure she'll tell you when she's ready." Elizabeth picked up the bills Polly had laid in front of her and squinted at the first one, which happened to be the electricity bill. Great heavens. Either the print on these things was getting a great deal smaller, or her sight was going. She'd have to wear glasses if things got any worse. That reminded her. "I don't suppose anyone's found Martin's glasses?"

"Not that I know of." Polly picked up another pile of bills and put them on Elizabeth's desk. "He's still not wearing them, anyway."

"I suppose we shall have to buy him new ones if we don't find them." Elizabeth's sigh was audible. "That will be more expense."

"I don't see why. He never looks through

them when he's got them on. They just sit on the end of his nose and he looks over the top of them."

"I know." Elizabeth smiled. "But I think he feels more secure when he's wearing them." She studied the girl poring over her desk. "Polly, did Marlene happen to mention exactly where this attack took place last night?"

"No, m'm. All I know is that it was on the coast road."

"Thank you, Polly." Elizabeth frowned at the electricity bill. The amount had increased alarmingly since the Americans had moved in. She would have to talk to the War Office and demand some kind of compensation.

"Which bills do you want me to pay, m'm?"

"Well, not this one, that's certain. At least not until we get the rent money in." Elizabeth quickly sorted through the pile, selecting the ones she thought could wait, then handed the rest to Polly. "You can pay these today. I'm going into the village for a while, but I should be back in plenty of time for lunch, if Violet should ask."

"Yes, m'm." Polly glanced at the bills in her hand. "I'll take care of these for you."

Elizabeth had to smile as she left the office. Who would have thought that an incompetent and sometimes lazy housemaid would turn into such a well-organized, efficient assistant. Polly had become quite indispensable.

While Elizabeth heartily supported Polly's

budding romance with Sam Cutter, and sincerely hoped that things would work out well for them, she knew that she would miss the child terribly if she should marry and move to America.

So many young women had such aspirations. One had to wonder how difficult it would be to settle down in a strange new country, far from home, family and friends, knowing no one except the man one had married, perhaps without really knowing him at all.

The overcast sky promised a shower or two as Elizabeth wheeled her motorcycle out of the stables. Desmond was nowhere to be seen, presumably weeding out the beds in the front of the manor. It was a never-ending task, according to her gardener, and one he detested. But like so many unpleasant things in life, one had to put up with them, and enjoy the simple pleasures while one could.

Good advice, Elizabeth mused, as she roared out of the driveway. But not always practical. Life could be very unfair indeed.

Instead of heading into the village, she took the coast road, and slowed her motorcycle down to cruising speed. The wind was quite fresh, and she was glad for the thick woolen cardigan she'd pulled on over her cotton frock.

Her hat, securely pinned to her hair, had a soft brim and tended to flap in her face at intervals. She attempted to adjust it with one hand while clinging to the handlebar with the other as

166

she rounded the curve. As always, she felt a rush of pleasure as the full sweep of the bay swept into view. Her attention divided between the pleasant vista and her wayward hat, she didn't see the object in the middle of the road until she was almost upon it.

With a violent twist of the handlebars, she narrowly missed what appeared to be a bed of nails. The change in direction mercifully shot her toward the ditch, rather than the edge of the cliffs, where she might well have hurtled clear through the railings to the beach sixty feet below.

As it was, the front wheel of her motorcycle plunged into the ditch, kicking up the sidecar, which dragged the whole contraption over onto its side.

Elizabeth landed with a thump on her rear that was most painful, even though she'd ended up on soft grass. Had it been the paved road she'd encountered with her rump, she thought ruefully, she might well have shattered her tailbone. Though even that seemed minor compared to what might have happened if she'd steered in the opposite direction.

Shaken by her narrow escape, she climbed out of the ditch. Thank heavens no one else was on that road at that moment. She would have presented a most inelegant sight. Hastily she straightened her skirt and brushed away the dirt and grass. Her hat had become dislodged, and she settled it firmly on her head, rearranging the pins to secure it.

The motorcycle was quite heavy, and it took some heaving and tugging to get it out of the ditch, but she finally managed it. Once she had it upright, she walked back to examine the object that had caused her mishap.

It was indeed, just as she had thought. A large piece of wood through which nails had been driven, presenting a nasty obstacle to any vehicle with tires. This must have been part of the attack last night on the American Jeep.

With a grunt of disgust, Elizabeth picked up the offending object and carried it back to drop it in her sidecar. This was evidence, and should be passed on to the authorities. She returned to the spot, and began searching the ground in a large area around where the booby trap had been left. Shards of glass and a few spots of blood were spattered several yards from where she'd encountered the nails, but other than that, there didn't seem to be anything else to provide a clue.

Obviously the damaged Jeep had been towed away, and the investigators had probably searched the area before her. Though one would suppose they would have disposed of the board of nails. Unless they missed it in the dark.

She was on her way back to her motorcycle when something shiny winked at her from the grassy verge. Pulse quickening, she hurried to the spot and knelt down in front of it. At first she couldn't see it, but as she moved back and forth she spotted a glimmer of light. Parting the grass, she reached for the object and drew it close to study it.

She recognized it immediately. She'd seen plenty of them before. It was a metal brooch, bearing spread wings beneath a crown, and the letters, RAF. Whoever had dropped this was a member of the Royal Air Force. British. Not American.

There was no rust on the pin. In fact, it looked shiny and new. Elizabeth pursed her lips as she turned it over in her hand. Perhaps it was a coincidence, but if so, it was a jolly big one. Her guess was that it had been dislodged from its wearer's jacket during the fracas that took place here. If so, it would seem that the three musketeers could well be British airmen.

She dropped the pin into the pocket of her cardigan and climbed aboard her motorcycle. This called for another visit to the Tudor Arms, and the sooner the better. At least there was some reason to give thanks. If the musketeers were guilty of poisoning their victims, it would seem they had given up that particular sport, at least for now. Perhaps Earl was right in his theory that the deaths had been more than the vigilantes had bargained for and they had ceased that outrageous form of harassment.

Nevertheless, four men had died. It was beginning to look as if these thugs were responsible, and they had to be stopped and punished for what they had done. Elizabeth lifted her chin, meeting the wind head on. She would not rest until she saw every one of them paying the price for their reckless and vindictive behavior.

Arriving at the police station a few minutes later, Elizabeth found George involved in an argument with Sid, who seemed to be getting the worst of the altercation.

"I told you until I'm blue in the face," George said, as Elizabeth entered the stuffy room. "I'm not a bleeding mind reader. If you don't tell me you're fed up with currant buns and want an Eccles cake instead, how am I supposed to know? I'm going to bring you bloody currant buns, aren't I. And now that I've paid for them you'll have to bloody eat them."

Since George had his back to the door, he failed to notice Elizabeth standing behind him. Sid, however, widened his eyes and jerked his head in a vain effort to alert George of their distinguished visitor.

"What's the matter now?" George demanded testily. "Having a bloody fit, are you?"

Sid shook his head, then blinked hard at George and jerked his head once more.

Catching on at last, George swung around. "Oh, begging your pardon, your ladyship. I didn't hear your motorcycle. Sort of crept up on me, you did." He sent a scowl at Sid that didn't bode well for the unfortunate man's morning. "What can I do for you, your ladyship?"

Elizabeth smiled encouragement at Sid, who winked rather crudely in return. "I was wondering if you had any information about the incident on the coast road last night," she said. "I'm really getting quite tired of these hooligans thinking they can come down here from London and disrupt our village in this horrendous manner."

George nodded vigorously. "You're right there, m'm. They're hooligans all right. Can't seem to catch 'em red-handed, though. They disappear before anyone can get their hands on 'em."

"What about the men who were beaten? Could they describe who did this to them?" She gracefully accepted the chair George pulled forward for her.

"No, m'm. Far as I know they couldn't." George waved at Sid, banishing him to the back room, then sat down behind his desk. "It were dark, so to speak, and one of the American blokes told me the assailants had scarves tied around their faces like bandits."

"Were they tall? Short? Did they speak? Did any of them have an accent?"

George stared at a pile of papers in front of him. "I don't know, m'm. Honest. The MPs were there and stopped the GIs from saying anything else." His voice took on a bitter note. "They left me to clean up after 'em, though."

"Well, you might have at least picked up the board of nails. I almost ran into it this morning."

George's eyebrows met above his nose. "I did pick it up, m'm. I brought it back with me and put it in the rubbish bin."

"Then there must have been two of them." She shook her head in disgust. "How did you happen to be there? I thought this happened late at night."

"Yes, m'm. It did. See, I heard about the punch-up and went up there on me bicycle. It were Jack Mitchem, the butcher who found them. He knocked me up to tell me what had happened. He was on his way back from Potter's farm with some chickens."

Elizabeth frowned. "Isn't that illegal? Chickens are on ration."

George winked. "That's why he were coming back late at night, m'm, weren't it."

Elizabeth decided to let that pass. "Well, tell me what you saw when you arrived at the scene."

George pursed his lips. "I'm not sure I'm at liberty to divulge that information, your ladyship."

Elizabeth sighed. "George, I really don't have time to play games this morning. Since the Americans are in charge of the investigation, it isn't your case, and therefore you can tell me whatever you want."

"I'm not sure there's going to be an investigation, m'm."

"No investigation?" She frowned at him. "Why not?"

George shrugged. "Well, before I went up there I rang the base to let them know what had happened. By the time I got up there, the

MPs were already there. They said it were probably a bunch of delinquents . . . ah . . . 'venting their frustration,' is how they put it. Said as how it happens all the time. They told me to clear up the road and they piled the GIs into the truck, tied the Jeep with a tow rope and they left."

Elizabeth puffed out her breath on a vexed sigh. "I see. Then we can expect no help from the American investigators."

George did his best to look innocent. "Help with what, m'm?"

"You know very well what." She paused, then keeping her tone as indifferent as possible, she added, "I don't suppose you noticed the color of the Americans' hair?"

George blinked. "Beg your pardon, m'm?"

"Their hair, George. What color was it?"

"I'm not sure I know what you're getting at, your ladyship."

"She wants to know what color their hair was!" Sid piped up from the back.

"I heard her, you nitwit!" George yelled back, then cleared his throat. "Sorry, m'm. That Sid gets on me blasted nerves sometimes."

"Quite." She raised her eyebrows at him. "Did you happen to notice the Americans' hair?"

"Can't say as I did, m'm. Is it important?"

"Not at all. I just wondered if you'd noticed, that's all." Deciding that she was getting in a little too deep, Elizabeth rose. "One way or another, I intend to find out the identity of these three musketeers, as they call themselves, and put a stop to all of this."

George's face registered alarm. "If they're down from London, m'm, they could be a bit hard to handle. Rough bunch, they are up there. It looks as if they're only after Yanks, so I say we should let the Yanks take care of it."

Elizabeth paused at the door and looked back at him. "These men are criminals, George. They are committing crimes against young men who are risking their lives to help us win this war. I will not tolerate such behavior in my village. If my father were here he would be the first to agree with me. Rest assured, I shall find out who they are, and when I do I expect you to do your duty and arrest them."

"Yes, m'm." George's expression clearly indicated his lack of enthusiasm.

"Oh, and speaking of arrests, I don't suppose you've heard anything from the inspector as to the whereabouts of that doctor in North Horsham?"

George blinked. "What doctor was that, your ladyship?"

Elizabeth sighed. "The man who was responsible for the death of the Adelaides' daughter. As far as I'm concerned, he's just as guilty of murder as is the person or persons who poisoned those poor men. I should think the inspector would be only too eager to apprehend him and put him in prison."

"I'm sure he is, m'm. I'll have a word with him about it next time I see him."

With another sigh, Elizabeth made her way back to her motorcycle. Conscious of George's earlier remarks about the noise the machine made, she'd parked it at some distance from the police station.

As she marched down the High Street, several people nodded and smiled at her in greeting. She acknowledged them with a regal wave of her hand. Her thoughts were concentrated on her conversation with George. As usual, it very much looked as if she was on her own with this investigation.

There was no doubt in her mind that she was dealing with some very dangerous individuals. She could only hope she was up to the task.

The clock in the town square chimed eleven times as she got on her motorcycle and rode down to the Tudor Arms. The ringing of the bells echoed across the valley, and a flock of crows answered the sound with harsh cries of their own as they swooped and dove among the tall poplars that lined the budding cornfields.

They reminded Elizabeth of the planes that took Earl into danger just about every day. She couldn't wait to see him that evening. She was looking forward to sharing a nice meal and a glass of her favorite cream sherry, talking about everything under the sun — everything except his life in America and the family awaiting his return.

That was a subject she had deliberately avoided ever since he'd told her that his marriage was not all it should be. She'd been unable to quell the faint hope that someday there might be a chance for them to be together. A false hope, nevertheless. Dwelling on the state of his marriage only fostered impossible dreams.

Still, she had to admit, even the faintest possibility lent excitement to life, which had become all too predictable until the War Office had commandeered her house for the American officers' quarters.

There were times when she wished she'd never met the handsome major, and compromised both her reputation and her heart. And then there were the other times, like right now, when she would not have missed the exquisite, tantalizing moments she'd spent with him. No man had ever made her heart race so, or had conjured up such enticing fantasies in her bewitched mind.

Violet was right. She was a fool. But oh, what joy to be foolish in the midst of all the adversity that surrounded her, to snatch those stolen moments and hold them forever in her memory. What was the quote? " 'Tis better to have loved and lost than never to have loved at all." Oh, how true. How very true. It was as if she could literally hear her heart singing as she soared into the fresh sea wind.

Chapter 11

In spite of the task awaiting her, Elizabeth's spirits were high as she entered the pub through the rear door. As she expected, Alfie was busy getting ready for the lunchtime customers. He seemed pleasantly surprised to see her back so soon, and sat her down with a glass of sherry at the deserted bar.

"What brings you back here, your ladyship?" he asked, as she sipped the burning liquid and allowed it to slide its delicious way down her throat.

She put down the glass and looked earnestly at him. "Alfie, I have a huge favor to ask of you."

He looked a little wary, but nodded all the same. "Anything for you, Lady Elizabeth. You can be sure of that."

"I assume you are acquainted with my house-maid, Sadie Buttons?"

"Yes, m'm. Sadie comes in here quite a bit. Got a good voice, she has. Gives us a song now and again on a Sunday night. The lads like her, too. She gives them a good game of darts, that girl."

Elizabeth smiled. "So I've heard. Anyway, she's coming here tonight with a young man. An

American. In view of recent events, I'd appreciate it very much if you would keep an eye on her. She's a very capable young lady, but one never knows, and I'd feel so much better if I knew someone was watching out for her."

Alfie nodded. "New boyfriend?"

"Something like that."

"Ah, well, I wouldn't worry too much, m'm. Most of the GIs are pretty decent chaps, just far from home and looking for a bit of company. There's a few bad eggs in the bunch, but so there is in our lads, too. They're few and far between. I'd say your Sadie'll do all right. You'll see."

"I'm not as much concerned about the Americans as I am these three musketeers that are causing so much trouble." She sipped some more of her sherry. "Did you hear what happened last night on the coast road?"

Alfie pulled out a cloth from under the counter and began wiping down the bar. "Yes, m'm. I did. Nasty business that. Everyone's going to breathe a little easier when they're caught, that's for sure."

"Well, at least they didn't kill anyone this time." Elizabeth glanced up at the clock. Any minute now the first visitor would be coming in. "Alfie, have you seen any RAF boys in here lately?"

Alfie looked surprised. "Can't say as I have, m'm. We get a lot of soldiers from the camp at Beerstowe, but I don't remember seeing any limey flyers around."

178

The familiar creak of unoiled hinges told Elizabeth that the first customer had arrived. She lifted her glass and drained it, smiling at Alfie as she set it back down. "That was lovely, Alfie. Thank you so much. You won't forget my little favor now, will you?"

"You can rely on me, m'm." He looked past her, to the man who had come up behind her to the bar. "Morning, Dick. What can I get for you this morning. Usual pint?"

Elizabeth felt a chill run down her spine. She'd been concentrating so much on the three musketeers, she'd completely forgotten about the Adelaides and their mysteriously missing daphne berries.

"You remember her ladyship?" Alfie said, as she turned to face the newcomer.

Dick Adelaide's face seemed carved in stone as he greeted her. "Your ladyship," he murmured, then turned to Alfie. "The usual mild and bitter, Alfie. Thanks, mate."

"Coming right up." Alfie reached for a glass tankard, stuck it under one of the pumps and pulled the brass handle. He filled the tankard half full of the dark brown liquid, then moved it under the next pump and topped it off with bitter ale. In typical barman fashion, he slapped the tankard down on the counter, sending a trickle of its foam collar down the sides of the glass. "That'll be a bob to you, mate," he said.

Dick Adelaide fished a shilling out of his pocket and laid it on the counter. "Cheap at half the price," he said, and lifted the tankard to his lips.

"Mr. Adelaide," Elizabeth said clearly, "I had the pleasure of meeting your wife the other day."

The man's cold eyes stabbed at her face. "Yeah, she told me your ladyship had come poking around."

Something about the way he'd said it gave her an unpleasant feeling. She stared him straight in the eye. "I realized I hadn't paid my customary call to a new resident. I'm not normally so tardy with my duties."

He gave her a brief nod that told her he didn't believe for one moment that her visit had been without purpose.

"Your wife told me all about your daughter's death." Elizabeth kept her gaze firmly on his face. "I'm so very sorry. It must have been an unbearable time for you both."

Alfie cleared his throat. "Another sherry, your ladyship?"

"Oh, no, thank you, Alfie." Elizabeth briefly transferred her gaze to the barman, and when she looked back, the venom in Dick Adelaide's eyes was unmistakable.

"We don't talk about it anymore," he said gruffly.

Elizabeth privately thought that both he and his wife would do a great deal better if they did talk about what happened more often. She kept silent on that score, however, saying quietly, "I quite understand. Losing a child must be the very worst tragedy anyone can suffer."

He seemed somewhat mollified by her genuine sympathy. He drank deeply from his glass, then muttered, "I blame that girlfriend of hers. Barb was never interested in the Yanks until Vera took her to the base. If it hadn't been for that little slut, my girl would still be alive."

Elizabeth's interest sharpened. "Vera?"

"Vera Stutworth. Lives down by the bay."

Of course, Elizabeth thought. The Stutworths. They had been tenants for almost two years now. Several children if she remembered correctly. She vaguely remembered the eldest daughter. That had to be Vera. Maybe she could tell her the color of Barbara Adelaide's boyfriend's hair. It was certainly worth paying her a visit. After all, even though Annie Adelaide had said her husband hadn't met Buddy, she wouldn't be the first wife to be ignorant about her husband's activities.

"By the way," she said, as Dick Adelaide started to leave, "I happened to notice some daphne bushes in your back garden. They appear to have lost their berries. I do hope you're not losing them to some dreaded disease."

The dairy farmer's face was inscrutable when he answered her. "I picked them off," he said. "They're deadly poison, and I didn't want the dogs eating them."

"Very wise," Elizabeth said evenly. She slid off her stool. "Well, I really must be going. Violet

181

gets so upset if I'm late for a meal. Do give my regards to your wife, Mr. Adelaide." Before he could answer, she waved at Alfie and hurried to the door.

Once outside she quickly mounted her motorcycle. Dick Adelaide's answer about the berries seemed feasible enough. Nevertheless, with any luck she could talk to Vera Stutworth that afternoon and find out if the elusive Buddy had red hair.

Though she would have to allow herself plenty of time to get ready for her dinner appointment with Earl. She wanted to look her very best for him. Her excitement intensified as she rode back to the Manor House. Dinner with Earl. What could be more exciting? Or more bittersweet?

Polly sat at her desk, taking great pains to copy down the rent amounts in a large ledger. She was proud of her neat columns of figures, and took great care to fit them inside the tiny boxes allotted to them. After each entry, she dipped her pen into the bottle of ink, shook it over the blotter to remove any drips, then wrote another amount down opposite a tenant's name.

She had almost reached the bottom of the page when the door flew open and Sadie hurtled into the room in her usual hurry. "Can't stop," she panted. "I've got another bathroom to do before lunch and I still haven't dusted in the great hall. The mighty knight will have dust up his nose if I don't get to his visor with me feather brush."

Polly grinned at her. "You talking about that rusty old suit of armor out there? It's a wonder it don't fall apart with you swiping at it with a feather duster every day."

" 'Ere, don't talk about my boyfriend like that. He's sensitive about his tin clothes, he is."

Polly burst out laughing. "You talk about him like he's real."

"Well, he is to me." Sadie slumped down on the chair behind her ladyship's desk. "After all, there was once a man inside that thing. I like to pretend there still is. Brightens up my dull day."

Polly shivered. "I hate that thing. I keep imagining a skeleton inside it."

"Well, anyway, tonight I'm going out with a real flesh-and-blood man." Sadie looked pleased with herself. "So how d'you like that?"

"You are?" Polly dipped her pen in the ink. "Who is he? The vicar?"

Sadie snorted. "Very bleeding funny, I'm sure. No, silly. I'm going out with a Yank, aren't I."

Polly's jaw dropped. "Go on! You don't like the Yanks. You said you'd never go out with one."

"I blinking play darts down the pub with them all the time, don't I?"

"That's different to going out with them."

"Yeah, well . . ." Sadie's voice trailed off.

Polly narrowed her eyes. Sadie had an awfully funny look on her face. "So what's so special about this one?"

"Oh, nothing." Sadie sent a deliberate glance at the clock. "I best be off. Violet will be howling at me if I don't get me jobs done before lunch."

"Wait a minute." Polly twisted around on her chair. "What's going on, Sadie Buttons?"

"Nothing." Sadie laughed, but it didn't sound like her usual laugh. "I just came in to tell you I'm going out with a Yank tonight. That's all."

"It's not the major, is it?"

Sadie's eyebrows shot skyward. "Major Monroe? Crikey, I should hope not. Her ladyship would have me guts for garters if I went anywhere near him." She danced over to the door. "Mind you, I'm not saying I wouldn't mind a turn around the mulberry bush with that one. Bit of all right, he is." Laughing, she went through the door and closed it behind her.

Polly sat frowning in frustration at the closed door. Sadie was keeping something from her, she could tell. What was the matter with everyone lately? What with Marlene keeping secrets and now Sadie, it seemed as if everyone else knew something she didn't.

It was bad enough that Sadie was hiding stuff from her, but when Marlene did it, that really hurt. Her own sister didn't trust her enough to tell her what was bothering her. Well, all right. She'd had enough. Tonight, before she went out with Sam, she was going to corner Marlene and demand to know what it was she was hiding. One way or another she was going to find out.

Having made up her mind on that score, Polly looked down at the ledger. An anguished cry burst from her lips when she saw the large blot of ink that had dripped onto the page. Thanks to Sadie and her secrets, she'd forgotten to shake her pen.

Carefully she used the corner of the blotter to soak up the offending bubble of ink. The whole page was spoilt. Now she'd have to write in the figures above the blot so as Lady Elizabeth could read them.

If it wasn't for her evening out with Sam, she'd bang her head against the wall. But then she only had to think about sitting in the dark cinema with his arm around her, and the whole world turned brighter. What did a blot of ink matter, when the one man who could make her truly happy was waiting to take her out? That's what really mattered. Nothing else. Absolutely nothing.

Having found out from Violet that Vera Stutworth worked at the wool shop in the High Street, that afternoon found Elizabeth again roaring into town on her motorcycle.

She parked it outside the town hall, where she could keep a fairly good eye on it, and crossed the street to the tiny shop that housed enough knitting wool to keep every woman in the village busy for years.

Knitting for the country's fighting men had become a large part of the war effort. Nearly every household had at least one woman sitting by the wireless at night busily clicking away with her knitting needles. Socks, gloves, jumpers, scarves and cardigans were turned out in huge numbers and sent overseas in the hopes of bringing some small measure of comfort to the armed forces.

Rita's Housewives League had achieved some splendid results with their knitting nights, while no doubt burning the ears of various villagers with their gossip. While Elizabeth, along with many residents of Sitting Marsh, viewed the league with wry amusement, she could not fault their contributions to a good cause.

She was not totally surprised to see Rita Crumm lurking inside the wool shop. In fact, had Elizabeth not been so intent on asking Vera a few questions, she would have returned to her motorcycle and delayed her visit until the coast was clear.

In any case, she was a little too late to retreat. Rita must have already spied her crossing the street. Her hunch proved correct. The woman was staring expectantly at the door when Elizabeth pushed it open with a loud jangling of the bell.

A very flustered young lady behind the counter greeted her, her words tumbling over themselves as she fumbled for the correct address.

Rita, on the other hand, had no such trouble. "Lady Elizabeth! I had no idea you could knit."

Somehow she'd managed to convey that Elizabeth was completely incapable of mastering such an intricate task. Elizabeth smiled sweetly at the young girl, who had finally managed to get out a breathless, "Good afternoon, your ladyship."

"Vera, isn't it? I believe we met some time ago. How are your parents? Well, I hope?"

"Very well, thank you, m'm." Vera looked as if she were about to faint.

Apparently annoyed at being ignored, Rita said loudly, "So what are you knitting then, Lady Elizabeth? A scarf?" Which was all Elizabeth could possibly manage, her tone implied.

"Actually I'm thinking of knitting a man's cardigan," Elizabeth said evenly. She reached out to finger a skein of maroon wool. "In double-cable stitch, with a purl border and ribbed hem." Once more she smiled at Vera. "Do you have a pattern for something like that?"

"I think so, m'm." Vera hurried out from behind the counter and paused in front of a shelf stocked with knitting patterns.

Well aware that double cable was a difficult stitch to master, Elizabeth beamed at Rita. "I do adore a challenge. Plain knitting can be so boring, don't you think?"

Rita looked as if she'd sucked a lemon. Picking up a large paper bag bulging with skeins in a variety of colors, she said stiffly, "Well, I wish you luck with your project. I shall look forward to seeing the completed garment."

"I'll be happy to show it to you," Elizabeth promised shamelessly, even though she knew she'd never have the patience to knit a cable-stitch cardigan. A year ago she'd started a plain jumper for Earl, and still had only completed the front and half the back. There were still the two sleeves to knit, as well as the neckband. She really needed to finish it, she chided herself. Perhaps in time to give it to him for a Christmas present.

Lost in a vision of presenting the finished jumper to him and imagining his response, she gave a start when Vera thrust a knitting pattern at her. "Here, your ladyship. Will this one do?"

Elizabeth peered at the picture on the front. It really was a very handsome cardigan. She could just see Earl wearing it, strolling with the dogs along the cliffs, sitting in the rocker in the conservatory while they laughed over something silly, or smiling at her across the dining room table, his vibrant gray-blue eyes intent on her face.

"I'll take it," she said abruptly. "And the wool as well. I like this color." She held up a skein of the maroon wool.

"Yes, m'm. I won't be a minute. I have to fetch some more from the back room."

Elizabeth gazed around the crowded shelves while she waited for Vera to reappear. Wool in every texture and color imaginable was crammed into the cramped spaces. Baby wool in pinks, blues, and the palest of yellow was stacked above a vivid array of purple, lavender, royal blue, holly red, kelly green, and the brightest rose pink imaginable.

Steel knitting needles from the slimmest number sixteen to the fattest number one sat above glass boxes of buttons in all shapes, sizes, and colors. Fascinating. Elizabeth caught sight of a polished ebony button that would look marvelous on the cardigan.

The chances of her attempting to actually knit the cardigan were remote, to say the least, nevertheless she felt compelled to purchase the buttons.

She waited until Vera had placed her purchases in a bag and had given her the change from her five pound note before saying lightly, "I bumped into Mr. Adelaide from the dairy farm this morning. He tells me you were a good friend of his daughter Barbara."

The young lady's pretty eyes clouded. "Yes, m'm. We were ever such good friends. I couldn't believe it when she died. I still miss her."

"I'm sure you do. Such a terrible loss at such a young age."

Elizabeth picked up her bag. "Did you ever meet her boyfriend? Ah, Buddy I think his name was?"

Vera nodded, her lips tightening. "No good, he was. Didn't care tuppence for Barbara. He just wanted a good time. I kept telling her that, but she wouldn't listen. It was all his fault. I knew he'd get her into trouble."

"I see. What a shame." Elizabeth moved toward the door. "I seem to remember seeing her with him. He had red hair, didn't he?"

Vera looked surprised. "No, m'm. Jet black hair, he had. Black eyes. Looked like he'd been sitting in the sun all the time. He was good-looking all right, but I never do trust the good-looking ones. They only want one thing, and they don't have no trouble getting it from some of the girls." She seemed to remember then to whom she was talking. "Sorry, m'm. I shouldn't be talking like that."

Elizabeth smiled. She liked Vera, she decided. Dick Adelaide was wrong about the girl. She was no slut. "Well, I'm sorry that you lost a good friend. They are hard to find."

"Yes, m'm. They certainly are."

Outside the shop, Elizabeth's smile faded. So Barbara Adelaide's boyfriend did not have red hair. It would seem her theory about Dick Adelaide looking for vengeance was wrong, after all. Which brought her back to the three musketeers. Unless it was simply a coincidence that all four men who died had red hair. Somehow, she just couldn't accept that. There had to be a connection somewhere. What was she missing?

The thing to do was find out if any of the

190

airmen involved in the fight last night had red hair. That might strengthen the notion that the color of the victim's hair was significant. Maybe Earl would know, or at least he could find out for her. She'd have to ask him.

In a hurry now to get back to the Manor House, she threw the bag into the sidecar. The board with the nails was still in there, too. She'd decided not to hand it over to George after all. If it should turn out to be evidence, she would give it to Earl to hand over to the American authorities. Though not right now. Obviously the Americans were not treating the incidents as seriously as she was, and until she had more proof, she'd just as soon not let them know she was investigating the problem.

In the meantime, she had her evening with Earl to look forward to, and for the time being, everything else ceased to matter. She intended to spend every moment completely focused on him, and everything else could wait until tomorrow. She could only hope that Sadie's evening was uneventful and perhaps even enjoyable. She didn't want anything to spoil this evening. Nothing at all.

Chapter 12

That evening Elizabeth regarded herself in the full-length mirror attached to the door of her wardrobe. She'd picked out a soft silk frock in royal blue with a heart-shaped neckline trimmed in tiny seed pearls. She'd fastened around her throat the double rows of pearls that had belonged to her mother, adding a sophisticated touch befitting the occasion. A light dash of lipstick, a final flick of a comb through her unbound hair, and she was ready.

She felt as if she were floating down the stairs to the dining room, her heart fluttering like leaves in the wind. She was halfway down when she realized that the front door was ajar. Martin's frail figure, jammed in the narrow opening, hid the visitor from view.

Wondering why he hadn't opened the door all the way, she continued down the stairs, expecting any minute to see Earl appear in the doorway. Martin was speaking in a low, urgent voice, as if afraid to be overheard.

Elizabeth sensed he wasn't talking to Earl after all, and crossed the entrance, curious to know the identity of the visitor. As she approached, she heard Martin mumbling and strained to hear the words.

"I would dearly love to invite you in, but I'm afraid your presence would arouse the wrath of Violet, and I'm quite sure madam would not approve."

A female voice answered him, her words muffled and indistinct.

"I would very much like to do that," Martin said, "but I'm at a loss as to how I would get there. It's too far to walk, I haven't ridden a bicycle in a good many years and short of pilfering madam's infernal bicycle machine I really have no way of —"

He broke off as Elizabeth reached him, apparently sensing her presence. Guilt was evident in his expression when he turned to her. "Good evening, madam. Please excuse me, I didn't hear you come down."

He still held the door partially closed, arousing Elizabeth's curiosity even further. "You have a visitor, Martin?"

The butler looked even more flustered. "No, madam, that is . . ."

"Yes, he does," the female voice answered firmly. "Good evening, Lady Elizabeth."

Martin swallowed, coughed, then very reluctantly, opened the door wider.

A rather dowdy woman stood on the doorstep, wearing glasses that looked remarkably like the ones Martin had lost. She clutched a large shopping bag to her chest, holding on to it as if in fear it would be stolen. "I'm Beatrice

193

Carr," the woman said with a faint note of defiance. "I'm a very dear friend of Martin's."

"That's . . . er . . . not exactly . . . er . . ." Martin's voice trailed off helplessly.

"It's all right, Martin." Elizabeth smiled at the woman. She had heard Violet mention Beatrice Carr on more than one occasion. Something about selling raffle tickets, if she remembered correctly. "Won't you come in?"

"Thank you, your ladyship." Beatrice moved closer to the door.

Martin, who appeared to be paralyzed with shock, still stood in her way.

Elizabeth gently prodded him until he moved backward.

Beatrice stepped inside the hallway, her eyes widening as she looked around. "Gracious, this is really posh." She peered up at the chandelier above her head. "That's awfully pretty, your ladyship."

"Thank you." Elizabeth turned to her speechless butler. "Martin, you may receive Miss Carr —"

"Mrs. Carr," Beatrice corrected. "Widowed, of course."

"Of course!" Martin shouted hoarsely, having finally found his voice.

Beatrice gave him a look from under her sparse eyelashes that was utterly coy.

Martin dissolved into a fit of coughing that quite alarmed Elizabeth. She patted him on the back, while Beatrice continued to gaze around

194

the hallway with a rather wistful look of enchantment on her lined face.

Martin finally recovered his breath and ceased coughing.

Elizabeth tried again. "As I was saying, Martin, you may receive Mrs. Carr in the library. I'll have Sadie bring up a pot of tea."

"Oh, I really can't stay, m'm," Beatrice said quickly. "I have to catch the bus back to North Horsham in a few minutes. I just came to bring Martin his raffle tickets, and then I'm off. I invited him to a social at our Women's Volunteers' club, but he says he can't get there."

"I don't think madam cares to hear about my predicament," Martin said stiffly.

"Nonsense, Martin. If you would like to go I'm sure we can arrange something," Elizabeth assured him. She caught Martin's eye, and saw desperation in them. A faint shake of his head convinced her. "Then again," she added hurriedly, "his duties do rather exclude any extended trips. Perhaps another time?"

Beatrice looked disappointed. "I'll think of something," she promised.

Martin's expression stated clearly that he sincerely hoped she wouldn't.

"Well, I must be off." Beatrice moved to the door, waiting pointedly for Martin to open it for her.

He did so with far more alacrity than usual, Elizabeth noticed.

Bidding them both good night, Beatrice stomped out of the door.

Martin barely waited long enough for her to clear the threshold before heaving the door closed behind her. "Thank goodness," he said, wiping imaginary sweat from his brow. "I thought we would never be rid of her."

"I was under the impression that you rather liked Mrs. Carr. You certainly defended her most gallantly when Violet mentioned her the other morning."

Martin shuffled his feet, teetering from side to side. "Yes, well, she is a charming woman, no doubt, but I would rather not invite her onto the premises. I'm quite sure Violet would be most unpleasant to her if she saw her."

Elizabeth studied his face. "Are you quite sure that's the reason you didn't want her to come in?"

"I can't imagine what you mean, madam."

"I mean, could the reason you didn't want her here be because she's wearing your glasses?"

Martin's face turned a dull red. "I was rather hoping you hadn't noticed."

"Yes, well, it would be a little difficult not to notice them. After all, the entire household has been searching for them for several days."

"Yes, I must apologize for that, madam." Martin hunched his shoulders, making him look even more aged than usual. "The truth is, I felt sorry for the woman. She sells the raffle tickets to help with the war effort, but her eyesight is so dismal she was finding it difficult to read the list of prizes available. Not only that, she was getting the tickets mixed up."

"So you gave her your glasses," Elizabeth shook her head. "Why didn't you tell us?"

Martin straightened his back as well as he could. "Can you imagine the tirade Violet would have given me every time she set eyes on me? I don't need the glasses, madam. Beatrice Carr does. She can't afford to buy them, so I gave her mine. She was most grateful."

"I'm sure she was," Elizabeth said dryly. "Very well, Martin, as long as you can manage without them. But if I find that you are having trouble getting around without them, I shall insist that she give them back to you."

"Yes, madam. Thank you, madam. Will that be all?"

"Not quite." Elizabeth glanced at the clock. "I'm expecting the major to join me for dinner. No doubt Violet has already informed you. I shall wait for him as usual in the conservatory."

"Oh, the major is already here." Martin began his long slow shuffle across the hallway. "He arrived some time ago. I showed him into the library."

Elizabeth uttered a little gasp of horror. So much time wasted that could have been spent with him. She sped across the hallway to the library and flung open the doors.

Earl sat in one of the armchairs, apparently engrossed in the book he held on his knees. He looked up as she hurried in, his smile banishing her dismay. "Hi," he said softly. "You look glamorous this evening."

Thoroughly flustered, Elizabeth flapped a hand to fan her warm face. "Thank you. I'm so sorry to keep you waiting."

"Not to worry. I've been enjoying this." He held up the copy of *A Farewell to Arms*. "Fascinating writer, that Hemingway."

"I quite agree." She sank on to the opposite armchair, her heart still warmed by his compliment. She couldn't remember anyone ever calling her glamorous before. "I understand the novel is largely biographical."

"Really?" He turned it over in his hands. "That makes it all the more interesting."

"Take it with you. I'm sure you'll enjoy it. It's an enthralling story." She was tempted to tell him how it ended, but managed to contain herself.

"Thanks, I'd like that. I'll give it back as soon as I've read it."

She nodded. "Are you hungry?"

"Starving." He looked at his watch. "I wanted to talk to you first before we go to the dining room. There's something you should know."

She felt a pang of apprehension. "Not bad news, I hope?"

"Well, kind of, I guess. I'm sorry to have to tell you, another of our guys died today."

"Oh, no." She put her hand over her mouth in distress. "Not more poisoning?"

"It looks like it." He put the book down on the table by his side and leaned back. "He was at the Tudor Arms earlier, got sick in the night and by this morning he was dead. Same symptoms as the other guys."

Elizabeth felt a chill. "It sounds as if the Tudor Arms could well be the source of the poison. What do your medics say?"

"Well. I haven't talked to them personally, but word on the base is that all military personnel have been warned not to eat or drink anything off the base unless they are quite sure it's harmless. They're considering declaring the Tudor Arms off limits."

"Oh, dear. This will upset Alfie and the owners of the pub. Not only that, it will hinder our efforts to apprehend the persons responsible. Then again, if the Americans don't drink the beer down there, they probably won't patronize the Arms, and the offenders will find another place to use their deadly poison."

"Unless they can prove the beer down there hasn't been tampered with."

"So your authorities at the base are treating the deaths as deliberate, then?"

He shrugged. "I guess so. I haven't heard anything about an investigation, but these guys can be pretty tight-lipped about what they're doing. What about you? Have you heard anything?"

She told him about the attack the night before, surprised to learn that he hadn't heard about it.

"They must not think it's connected," he said, when she was finished. "Or they would have put it in the report."

"I was wondering if either of the fellows who were beaten had red hair," Elizabeth said. "Could you possibly find out?"

He frowned. "Now that you mention it, the guy who died this morning had red hair."

Elizabeth hissed out her breath. "Then it appears there might be a connection after all. I thought as much."

"I don't know about the guys who got beat up last night." Earl looked worried. "You really think these musketeer guys are behind all this?"

"Well, I found out that the man Dick Adelaide's daughter was going out with didn't have red hair, so that rather lets him out of the picture, so to speak, don't you think? Though I suppose it could still all be a huge coincidence."

"I don't know." Earl's brow crinkled in frustration. "It seems such a lousy reason to kill someone, just because he has red hair."

"And is American," Elizabeth reminded him.

"Yeah, that too. But lots of folks have it in for us, so that's easier to understand. Though I don't think anyone's taken it this far before."

"Well, we'll have a better idea when we know if any of the men involved in last night's incident have red hair. If at least one of them does, I think we can conclude that these men could well be targeted by the infamous three musketeers."

"For whatever reason," Earl murmured. "I'd sure like to know the answer to that one."

"Whatever the reason, these men have to be apprehended. Even if they're not responsible for the deaths, they've already caused enough harm and damage to have criminal charges brought against them."

"I agree with that. I'll have a word with the MPs at the base. Though they're probably already looking for them."

"Oh, would you?" Elizabeth smiled at him in relief. "I'd feel better if I knew something is being done about them."

"I'm not promising anything. So far our guys are playing this whole thing down. But now that someone else has died, they might just figure they have enough to go ahead with a full investigation. If our little decoy plan works, we might even get our hands on the bad guys tonight."

"I certainly hope so. I hope Sadie and that nice young man she's with don't come to any harm. I feel quite concerned about them."

"Try not to worry too much about them. Joe Hanson is a very capable young man and he'll take real good care of Sadie. I promise you."

"Yes, well, all I can say is that I'll be happy to see her return. I just hope that this plan works and we can catch the culprits." A thought made her pause. "What will Lieutenant Hanson do if he does see something suspicious? I hope he's not planning to take on three men single-handedly?"

Earl shook his head. "He has orders to call the base from the pub. I've already cleared it with Alfie. The MPs can be there very shortly, and they'll question the suspects and if necessary, take them back to the base."

"Well," Elizabeth murmured, somewhat reassured, "I suppose that will be all right then." She slid off the chair and smoothed down her skirt. "In the meantime, why don't we find out what Violet has cooked up for us tonight."

"Sounds like a good idea." He joined her at the door and linked her arm in his. "Lead the way, your ladyship. I'm more than ready."

So was she, Elizabeth thought wryly. Though not necessarily for the meal. Inwardly scolding herself for her lascivious thoughts, she proceeded with him to the dining room.

Sadie clung to Joe's arm as they walked through the door of the pub, determined to play the part of a loving girlfriend to the hilt. The fact that Joe seemed uncomfortable with the pretense only made her all the more anxious to put on a good show.

At least one of them would have to make it look good, and judging by the way Joe held himself as stiff and straight as a telephone pole, it was all going to fall on her.

In fact, she was a little miffed that he wasn't enjoying it as much as she'd hoped. All right, so it was all pretense in order to catch the mean blokes what were causing all this trouble, but he could at least make the effort to look as if he were having a good time. She felt like she was dragging him around with her like a sack of moldy potatoes.

Seating herself on one of the bar stools, she grinned at Alfie, who winked back at her. "I'll have me usual, luv," she called out.

Alfie nodded, finished serving the British soldiers lounging at the end of the counter, then poured a gin and orange for her. Setting it down in front of her, he glanced at Joe. "All right, mate. What'll it be?"

"Beer," Joe said. He stared into the long mirror that lined the back of the bar. "Make it a pint of bitter."

"Coming up." Alfie poured the beer and set the foaming tankard on the counter. Joe handed over a pound note and waited for his change.

"Don't seem as busy tonight." Sadie glanced around. "Want a game of darts?"

"I don't play darts." Joe kept staring at the mirror.

Sadie stared at it, too, but couldn't see anything except the reflection of the room behind them. One of the Yanks was at the piano, playing a bloody awful version of "A Nightingale Sang in Berkeley Square." A bunch of his mates stood around the piano, trying to sing along. None of them knew the proper words and the stuff they were using to replace them was enough to make a sergeant major's hair curl.

Near the piano a bunch of old women sat with their heads together, trying to be heard above the din. Sadie recognized a couple of them from the Housewives League. Bleeding joke that lot was. Wasting their time hanging around the cliffs waiting for the invasion. If the Nazis ever did invade, what did a bunch of silly women think they were going to do? Beat them off with a frying pan?

Sadie turned her attention to Joe. "Tell me about where you live in America," she said, reaching for her glass.

He flicked a glance at her, then stared back at the mirror. "Minneapolis."

She was none the wiser. She had no idea where the heck Minny-whatever-he'd-said was. Could have been at the end of the world for all she knew.

Two gins later, she still didn't know much more about him. Her frustration was beginning to make her mad. She didn't want to be mad at Joe. She liked him. But if he kept on ignoring her like this, nobody in the pub would think they even knew each other, leave alone were going out.

Deciding it was time to get things moving, Sadie pushed her empty glass across the counter. "I'll have a shandy, Alfie," she called out.

This at least got Joe's attention. "What's a shandy?" he asked, taking his eyes off the mirror for once.

"It's half beer, half lemonade." She smiled up at him and flapped her eyelashes, which had been heavily coated with Vaseline. "It's lighter for a lady to drink."

He didn't answer her, but coughed up the money and went back to staring at the mirror.

Sadie, feeling just a little tipsy from drinking the gins too fast, leaned toward him. " 'Ere, you are supposed to be my boyfriend, you know."

Joe swivelled his gaze to her face and then back to the mirror again. "I'm buying you drinks, aren't I?"

Sadie pulled back. "I don't know what bleeding for. You're acting as if you hate me."

"I don't hate you." He lowered his voice and spoke out the corner of his mouth. "I'm just concentrating on doing my job."

Leaning toward him again, Sadie whispered fiercely, "Your job is to make these blokes in here think we're potty about each other. They're not going to think that if you act like I've got some 'orrible disease, now are they."

Joe shifted his weight on the bar stool so that he was an inch or two closer. "Is that better?"

"Not really." Sadie sighed. "Haven't you ever had a girlfriend?"

She was intrigued to see a dull red flush on his cheeks. "Of course I have," he said stiffly.

She leaned into him so that her bosoms pressed against his arm. "Go on. Bet you haven't."

He pulled away from her as if he'd been shot.

"I'm just not used to being fresh with a stranger."

"Well, if you got to know me a little better, I wouldn't be such a stranger, would I." She drank down some of the shandy, and put her glass down next to his nearly full one. "Come on, luv. Drink up. Maybe it'll loosen you up."

"I have to stay alert," Joe muttered, his lips barely moving.

"Oh, I think I can keep you alert, all right." Sadie's laugh gurgled out. "Just leave it to me."

Joe looked as if he was going to be sick. "Er . . . why don't we just talk."

"You're no bloody fun, you know that? What's the matter with me, then? Am I that ugly?"

"No, no," Joe assured her hastily. "You're . . . er . . . real pretty . . . I mean . . . you're a nice-looking woman. I think . . . er . . . any man would be . . . happy to be going out with you."

Sadie grinned. "Well, now, that's more like it." She leaned toward him. "Give 's a kiss, then."

Joe's eyes widened. "What? Oh, no. Not in front of everyone. No. I'm supposed to be . . ." he sent a haunted look at the mirror.

Disappointed, Sadie reached for her glass again. She wasn't going to chase him. If he wanted to be like that, well, it was his loss. But he certainly wasn't much of an actor. This whole evening was becoming a bit of a drag.

Maybe if she got him interested in talking about something it might loosen him up a bit. She pounced on a subject she thought might fascinate him. "Ere," she said, nudging his elbow. "Guess who I saw the other day."

Unfortunately, Joe had his glass in his hand and some of his beer spilt on his sleeve. It seemed to upset him a lot. He pulled a handkerchief from his pocket and began dabbing it until she thought he'd put a hole in the darn thing.

"Winston Churchill," she announced, in a last-bid attempt to gain his attention. "I saw Old Winnie walking along the cliff tops, bold as brass. I said hello to him and he doffed his hat at me, he did."

She'd succeeded in her mission. Joe's hand stilled while he stared at her. "You saw Winston Churchill?"

Delighted to have finally caught his interest, she ignored the blatant disbelief in his voice. "Right there in front of me, he was," she declared with pride. "Almost ran him over with me bike, I did."

Joe's frown drew his fuzzy ginger brows together. "Are you nuts?"

That did it. It was bad enough that no one believed she'd seen the prime minister, but to call her bonkers was hitting below the belt. She picked up her glass and drained it in several loud gulps, then set it down hard on the counter.

Gathering up her purse, she said frigidly, "I think I'm going home now. You can look for the nasty buggers yourself. You don't need me."

Joe's mouth opened and closed, though nothing came out of it.

Sadie slid off the stool then stepped closer until she was right up against him. "Just in case they're in here and watching us," she said, making her voice low and husky like the film stars did, "Here's something to remember me by." With that she pressed her lips firmly against his, held them there for a second or two, then without waiting to see his reaction, marched out of the pub, amid a chorus of wolf whistles.

Chapter 13

Polly was in front of the mirror, doing her best to make herself look older with lipstick and rouge, when Marlene barged into the bedroom and flung herself on the bed.

"Where you going all dolled up like a Christmas tree?" she demanded. "You going down the pub again?"

"No I'm not." Polly added a dab of rouge to her cheeks and sat back to study the results. "I'm going to the pictures in North Horsham."

"By yourself?"

"Course not by meself." Deciding that she looked too much like a clown, Polly scrubbed her cheeks with her face flannel. "I'm going with Sam, aren't I."

"Go on!" Marlene bounced upright, making the bedsprings groan in protest. "When did this happen, then?"

"He asked me out yesterday." Polly drew the lipstick carefully across her top lip, then mashed her lips together to spread it evenly. "I would have told you last night but you were out." She swung around in her chair. "Where were you, anyway? You got a new boyfriend?"

Marlene laughed. "Not on your life. I've had

it with boyfriends. I've got more important things to think about, haven't I."

Polly studied her older sister. Marlene's creamy skin seemed to be glowing, and her eyes were dancing with excitement. She hadn't seen Marlene this lit up about something in ages. "What's going on?" she demanded. "I know something's up. Why won't you tell me? What's the big secret?"

"It's not a secret anymore." Marlene swung her legs to the floor and began dancing around the room. "Everyone's going to know about it soon."

Polly felt a stab of alarm. "You're not in the family way, are you? Ma will kill you. If our dad doesn't get to you first."

Marlene laughed and dropped onto the bed once more. "No, silly. It's nothing like that. I've joined up, haven't I. I'm going to be an ambulance driver."

Polly felt as if someone had thrown a bucket of cold water at her. "What, in London? In all them air raids? You'll get killed."

"Better than that." Marlene grinned happily at her. "I'm going to the battlefield. I'm going abroad. I don't know where yet. It might be France, or even Italy. Just think. Me, Marlene Barnett, driving around Italy."

Unexpected tears spilled unheeded down Polly's cheeks. "No, Marl, you can't go! Ma won't let you go!"

"She can't do nothing about it. I joined up,

didn't I." Marlene got up from the bed and put her arms around her sister. "Don't cry, Polly. I'll be all right. They don't bomb ambulances. I'll be safer than anyone else out there."

"But why?" Polly wailed. "Why'd you want to leave Ma and me and go away?"

"I'm going crazy washing people's hair all day." Marlene went back to the bed and sank down. "I keep hearing the news on the wireless about all those men out there getting hurt and I keep thinking, what if it was our dad? I'd want someone to be there to help him. Then I got thinking about how great it would feel to be the one helping him, and all the other blokes out there, and one thing led to another and I ended up signing up."

Polly gulped down a sob. "But you don't know how to drive an ambulance!"

"Well, I had a taste of it when I met Pete that time. You remember, the newspaper reporter from London? He showed me how to drive his car and I liked it. Ever since then I kept dreaming about driving me own car. And now I'll be driving all the time and I'll be doing something for our boys overseas as well."

Polly suddenly realized that Sam was picking her up in about twenty minutes and if she didn't stop crying she'd have red swollen eyeballs. She snatched a handkerchief out of her dresser drawer and blew her nose. "Have you told Ma?"

"I told her just now." Marlene's grin faded. "She cried, too."

"I should think so." Polly looked hopefully at her sister. "What if you change your mind? Can you get out of it?"

"Not once you sign up." Marlene got up again and took the handkerchief out of Polly's hand. "I don't want to get out of it, Polly. I'm not going to change my mind so you might as well get used to it. Now let's see if we can make you pretty for Sam."

Polly did her best to recapture the excitement she'd felt about being with Sam, but it was hard. Marlene's news had put a damper on the evening. She just hoped she could forget it long enough to enjoy her time with him. She just couldn't believe that Marlene was leaving home and going into terrible danger where all the fighting was. Right now, she needed Sam more than ever before.

Second Lieutenant Joe Hanson finished his beer and glanced at his watch. Almost closing time. He'd wasted a whole evening sitting at a bar when he could have been training in the ring. These guys weren't going to show, and what's worse, he'd upset a very nice young lady. It wasn't her fault he'd panicked when she started coming on to him. She was right about one thing. He hadn't had a girlfriend. Not a real one anyway. Most of the girls he'd taken out spent one evening with him and decided he wasn't fast enough for them.

Joe hauled himself off the stool and headed

for the door. Trouble was, he wasn't like most of these guys. He was shy, especially around girls. They made him nervous, and when he got nervous he stuttered. Just because he was good at boxing, girls expected him to act like Clark Gable, when he felt more like Jimmy Stewart. He wished he could be more passionate with a girl, but every time he thought about it, his insides started twisting around and his hands started shaking and it was all he could do just to put his arm around her.

Joe pushed the door open and stepped outside into a cool night breeze. After the haze of smoke inside, it smelled good. Nice and fresh.

He started across the car park to where his Jeep was parked, and was almost there when he heard a quiet moan. The moon was partly hidden by a passing cloud and it was too dark to see properly.

Squinting into the darkness, Joe called out, "Is someone there?"

A wavery woman's voice wafted out of the shadows. "I'm here. I think I've twisted my ankle."

He headed in the direction of the voice. The moon slid out from behind the cloud and he saw her. She was sitting on the ground, her hands clutched around one of her ankles. To his relief she was old, like his mom. For a moment he'd been afraid it was one of the local young girls waiting to trap a GI. He didn't want to be rude to someone else.

Reaching the woman, he held out his hand. "Can you stand?"

"I think so."

She had a surprisingly strong grasp for an old woman. He hauled her to her feet and watched while she tried her weight on the ankle. When she cried out and stumbled, he grabbed her arm. "Where do you live? How are you getting home?"

"I was going to walk." She looked up at him, the pale moonlight making her wrinkles stand out like cracks in an eggshell. "I don't think I can, though."

"My Jeep is over here. I'll take you home."

She started to protest, but he insisted, gently steering her across the car park in the murky darkness. He got her into the passenger's seat with a bit of pushing and shoving, then rounded the hood to his own seat.

The engine split the silence with a loud roar, and they were off. She uttered a small shriek, as if startled by the speed, and he slowed down a little. "You'll have to tell me how to get there."

"Oh, it's not far. Just down this road until you reach the crossroads, then turn left." He sensed her looking at him. "What's your name, young man?"

He told her, then good manners compelled him to add, "So what's your name?"

"I'm Maisie Parsons. This is so awfully good of you. I don't know how I would have got home without you."

He nodded, unwilling to carry on a conversation. It was too hard to be heard over the roar of the engine. The wind caught them head on as they rounded the curve and he glanced at her. "You might want to hold on to your hat. You could lose it in this wind."

She lifted a hand and clutched the felt hat she wore. She didn't say anymore until they were about half a mile down the lane, and she pointed to a row of cottages set back off the road. "There," she shouted. "Third one down."

He slowed to a halt and cut the engine. "Wait there and I'll help you out."

She gave him her hand again and he helped her down, then waited at her door until she found her key. "Thank you again, Lieutenant. This was most kind of you. I'd like to give you a little something for your trouble."

"No, ma'am. Thank you, but that's not necessary." He started backing away. "I'm just glad to help. You take care of yourself. Good night."

"Oh, no, I insist." She'd sounded really upset and he paused. "I'd never forgive myself if I let you go off empty-handed after you've been so very kind. Please, just wait here. I won't be a moment."

Considering she was in pain, she hopped inside the house pretty fast. He waited, hating to take anything from her, yet reluctant to just walk away. His mother had raised him to respect his elders.

The old woman reappeared in a matter of minutes, carrying a tin box in her hands. "Here," she said, thrusting it into his hands. "It's my specialty. The best gingerbread you've ever tasted. Anyone in the village will tell you so."

He took the tin from her, feeling awkward. "Well, thank you, ma'am. I sure appreciate this."

"It's the least I can do. I hope you enjoy it." She started to close the door, then added, "Don't share it with anyone, or they'll all be at my door clamoring for my gingerbread."

He smiled. "I promise, ma'am. I'll eat it all myself."

"Good. Good." She nodded. "Well, good-bye, young man."

"Night, ma'am." Touching his cap, Joe turned away and headed back to the Jeep. He felt better. His encounter with Sadie Buttons had left him feeling guilty, and doing something nice for that old lady had helped ease his conscience.

He climbed into the Jeep and laid the tin on the seat next to him. Gingerbread. Make a great midnight snack. With a roar, he took off into the night.

Maisie Parsons heard him go. And she was smiling.

Polly sat in the darkened cinema, fighting a bout of acute resentment. Although she'd pressed herself against Sam's arm throughout the whole film, he hadn't made one move to put his arm around her.

She tried to tell herself it was because they weren't in the back row. To her intense disappointment, Sam had headed down to the middle of the aisle before ushering her into the seats on the edge of the row.

Having already seen the film once, her attention wandered, focusing on various visions of her life with Sam in America. She saw herself sailing across the ocean and arriving in New York, right in front of the Statue of Liberty. She knew all about that from the films.

She saw herself sitting by a swimming pool under a palm tree, or riding a lift up one of those tall buildings. She saw a house and a big garden, lots of trees and flowers. She saw herself driving a big car down a winding road toward the ocean.

That reminded her of Marlene and her news about being an ambulance driver. She didn't want to think about that. Not tonight. Not when she was with Sam.

She glanced up at him. He'd made her sit on his good side, so she couldn't see the scars from there. He looked like the old Sam, the laughing, joking Sam who'd made her so happy. The Sam who had bought her presents and teased her and kissed her good night.

But that was before the accident. Before he'd found out she'd lied about her age. Before he'd started treating her like a little girl instead of a grown woman, the way he had before.

Her heart ached to have those days back

again. He looked so stern now, so miserable. And she didn't know how to get the old Sam back.

The lights came up, dazzling her. She hadn't realized the film had ended. She stood up for the national anthem, standing to attention as they played "God Save the King." Sam stood at her side, and she could almost feel the wall he'd put up between them.

She followed him out of the cinema, her heart thumping with apprehension. Something told her this wasn't an evening out for pleasure. Something was wrong. Sam just wasn't acting the way a boyfriend does when he takes out his girl.

She sat silently by his side as they roared along the main road back to Sitting Marsh, then headed along the coast road. She expected him to drive her straight home. She was already bracing to hold back the tears until she reached the safety of her bedroom. There was no way she was going to let on how miserable she was.

Then again, there was always the hope he'd kiss her good night. A very tiny hope, she had to admit. Maybe she could take him by surprise and plant one on his lips. Then he'd start re-membering what a lovely time they used to have and he'd kiss her back and . . .

She was startled when Sam braked and came to a screeching stop on the grass verge over-looking the beach. The silence, after the loud roar of the engine, seemed strange. She waited, her heart thudding against her ribs so hard she could feel the vibration right through her blouse and cardigan.

He didn't say anything for the longest time. Just about the moment she thought she would scream from the awful anxiety, he turned to her. Her heart skipped. This was it. Somehow she knew that what he was about to say would govern the course of her life forever. This was a moment that would live in her memory for a lifetime. She fastened her gaze on his face and waited for him to speak.

"I have to be getting back to the base," Earl said, as he rose from the rocking chair. "It's getting late."

"It is, indeed." Elizabeth glanced at the small ornate clock on the table at her side. "I had no idea it was so late." They had been enjoying a glass of sherry in the conservatory, and she hadn't realized the time passing by on its inevitable march forward. These moments were so precious to her. And so very fleeting.

He grinned. "Time flies when you're having fun." He held out his hand. "This has been real nice."

"I've enjoyed it, too." She rose swiftly, putting her hand in his. "Thank you for joining me for dinner. It was a lovely evening."

"The pleasure's all mine, believe me. Violet outdid herself tonight. That meat pie was real good."

"Well, she'll be the first to admit she's not the most accomplished of cooks, and the rationing makes things even more difficult." Elizabeth accompanied him to the door. "But now and again she really puts herself out and the results can be quite surprising."

"Hey, I'll take one of Violet's home-cooked meals over the chow in the mess hell anytime."

She smiled at that. "Take care of yourself, Earl."

"Yeah. I'll let you know if Joe turned up anything at the pub."

"And I'll talk to Sadie. I think we would have heard by now though if anything significant had happened."

"Yeah, you're probably right. Guess we'll have to try again sometime." He looked down at her hand for a moment, then turned it palm down and brought it to his lips.

He'd kissed her hand before, but this time the gesture seemed to be more intimate, more disturbing. She withdrew her fingers, afraid he would feel them trembling. The tremors didn't stop until long after he'd left the room.

Knowing she wouldn't sleep until her qualms about Sadie had been eased, Elizabeth hurried down the steps to the lower hallway on her way to bed and paused outside of Sadie's room. Her light tap on the door was answered almost immediately.

Sadie was in the process of getting ready for bed. With her face scrubbed clean and her hair scraped back and wound around a host of metal curlers, she looked young and immensely vulnerable. She was obviously shocked to see Elizabeth and clutched her dressing gown around her throat as she stared at her.

"Is something the matter, m'm?" she asked fearfully. "It's not the invasion, is it?"

"Good Lord, no." Elizabeth put out a hand and patted her arm. "I'm so sorry, I didn't mean to startle you. I was just concerned about how things went tonight."

Sadie's lips tightened. "Well, I tell you, m'm, if you were hoping to trap them musketeers into trying something on Joe because he was with me, I'm afraid it ain't going to work. Joe acted as if I had the bleeding plague. No one down there would ever believe we were going out together."

"Oh, dear." Elizabeth could read the disappointment in Sadie's eyes. "What happened?"

"Nothing! That's the point. Maybe I'm not his type. I dunno. He seemed friendly enough yesterday afternoon when we were talking about it, but when it came down to us getting cozy in public, he jumped back like a horse from a firework. I finally gave up and left him in the pub."

Elizabeth clicked her tongue. "I'm sure he didn't mean to do that. Perhaps he's just a little shy."

Sadie shrugged. "P'rhaps. Whatever it was, I don't think it did any good down there. I'm sorry, m'm. I didn't mean to let you down."

"You didn't let me down at all," Elizabeth assured her. "I shouldn't have asked you to do this. I had my doubts about it from the beginning. I should have listened to them."

"Aw, that's all right, m'm. I got an evening out, didn't I. No harm done."

"Well, thank you, Sadie. I'll let you get some sleep now." Elizabeth heard the door close as she walked back up the hallway to the kitchen. Poor Sadie. Her pride had received a nasty blow. Elizabeth felt a moment's anger toward the young lieutenant who had acted so thoughtlessly. Her opinion of him had gone down considerably.

It was just as well the three musketeers had not paid a visit to the Tudor Arms that night. Elizabeth wasn't at all sure that Lieutenant Joe Hanson would have had the gumption to protect her companion from harm.

The problem was, she was no closer to finding out the identity of these dangerous criminals, and until they were apprehended, that meant every red-headed American in the vicinity of Sitting Marsh was in danger. It was a sobering thought.

Polly shivered in the cool draft that wafted around the back of her neck. She wasn't sure if it was the ocean breeze, or the look on Sam's face that made her feel so cold.

She could see him clearly in the moonlight, his scars barely visible in the soft glow. His eyes were sad, though, and he had trouble looking at her. Her spirits sank all the way to the ground.

"Polly," he said, his voice hushed with pain. "I never meant to hurt you. I thought we could have a good time together, without either one of us getting in too deep."

Her lips were so dry she had difficulty making them move. "You never meant to marry me," she said dully.

He looked away, across the ocean. "I cared for you a lot. I enjoyed being with you. You're a wonderful girl, Polly. Someday you'll find someone else and you'll make him a great wife. He'll be a very lucky man to have you."

"I don't want anyone else!" The words had burst out of her, louder than she'd meant them to, and they seemed to echo all the way down the lonely beach. She wouldn't cry, she told herself fiercely. She would not let herself cry. "I want *you*," she whispered quietly. "I could make you a good wife, Sam. Just give me the chance."

"You wouldn't be happy in the States, Polly. It's not like England —"

"Yes, I would!" She clutched his sleeve. "I could be happy anywhere as long as I was with you."

"Polly —"

"You don't have to decide right now, Sam. Let's just go out together, the way we used to. You said yourself we had a good time together."

"Polly —"

"I won't nag you about getting married, I promise. I'll just be happy to go out like we did before and —"

"Polly, listen to me."

Something in his voice stopped her flow of words. She put her hand over her mouth to hold back a sob.

"Polly," Sam's voice broke, then he cleared his throat. "They're shipping me back stateside," he said quietly. "I leave next week. I won't be coming back here."

"N-o-o-o-o!" The word bubbled out behind her hand. She was crying after all. Helpless, hopeless tears that rolled down her cheeks and splashed onto her arm. "I . . . c-can't live without you, Sam! Take me with you. I can't go on without you."

"Yes, you can." His voice harsh now, he turned to her. "Polly, you deserve someone better than me. You deserve a man who will love you the way you need to be loved. You're young and you have your whole life in front of you. You don't need me. You can do so much better."

Words, she knew now, would be a waste of time. She could never make him understand. He would never know how much she loved him, and would go on loving him until the day she died. Even if he had broken her heart.

She just wanted to die.

Everyone was deserting her. Marlene, and now Sam. She felt as if the whole world had landed on her shoulders, pressing her into the ground. Her life was over. She would never ever be happy again. She might as well join the convent and be a nun.

Chapter 14

If there was one thing guaranteed to start Elizabeth's day off on the wrong foot, it was to run into Rita Crumm. Anywhere. What compounded it was to confront that lady in the normally peaceful confines of Bessie's bake shop.

Elizabeth had attended a committee meeting of the town council that morning, to discuss the summer garden fête at the vicarage. An annual event, it was the subject of a great deal of anticipation for the villagers of Sitting Marsh.

The tradition dated back several hundred years, to when the fête was actually a summer marketplace, where various merchants traded their wares. Over the centuries it had gradually transformed into the modern-day version of a garden fête, and had been moved from the town square to the vicarage, where the assorted stalls could display their offerings amid the delightful gardens full of summer blossoms.

Last year Elizabeth had judged the local talent contest, with the help of a somewhat reluctant Earl. She remembered it as one of the nicest days she had spent in his company, and was looking forward to repeating the pleasure this year.

She was relieved to learn that she had been released from her duty as contest judge, no doubt because she had chosen a young child as the winner in favor of Rita's horrendous presentation of the Housewives League.

She happily agreed to judge the bake sale this time around. She was rather looking forward to persuading Earl to assist in the task. Not that she expected much reluctance on his part.

Earl had long and quite loudly extolled the virtues of English baked products. He was particularly partial to buttered scones, layered with Devonshire cream and strawberry jam, a treat that was hard to come by in these days of rationing.

Staring at the plate of Chelsea buns in front of her now, she smiled in anticipation. Yes, Earl would enjoy helping her judge the bake sale. In her mind she could see him now, tasting the buns, tarts, pies, pastries and cakes with that expression of sheer bliss that she found so endearing.

Engrossed in her daydream, she was startled when a familiar voice banished her thoughts.

"Lady Elizabeth. I wonder if I may join you for a few minutes?"

Looking up into the sharp features of her nemesis, Elizabeth forced a smile. "Good morning, Rita. Please, sit yourself down."

Rita Crumm lowered herself onto the edge of the chair as if it were smothered in horse dung. "Thank you. I happened to run into Captain

Carbunkle this morning. He tells me he's planning a wedding."

"Yes. Isn't that divine?" Elizabeth kept her smile firmly fixed on her face, while she wondered what the real reason could be for Rita's intrusion on her pleasant morning. "He tells me he's marrying Priscilla Pierce. Such a surprise."

"Not really." Rita sniffed. "They've been carrying on in secret for months."

Elizabeth bit her tongue. Priscilla had confided in her several months ago about her association with Wally Carbunkle, and Elizabeth had promised to keep it secret. She might have known Rita would ferret it out. Nothing escaped that woman's sharp nose.

"Anyway," Rita said, "That's not what I wanted to talk to you about, your ladyship. I also heard that you will be judging the bake sale at this year's fête."

Elizabeth promptly lost her appetite. As far as she knew, Rita was as incompetent at baking as she was at nearly everything else. "Yes," she said carefully. "I have agreed to judge the bake sale, but —"

"I just wanted you to know that the members of the Housewives League will be entering their baked goods as usual, and would like to donate whatever's left to the American base. I was wondering if you'd ask that major of yours if that is all right with everyone. We always have so much left over, it's a shame for it all to go to waste. Especially since the Americans are kind enough to help us out with the ingredients."

This was news to Elizabeth, but she wasn't entirely surprised. A great deal of trading went on between the villagers and the American airmen. Deciding to ignore Rita's allusion of intimacy between the major and herself, Elizabeth said pleasantly, "I'm quite sure the men will be delighted with the offer, but I will certainly confirm it with Major Monroe."

"Thank you, your ladyship. Maisie Parsons has already offered to make an extra batch of gingerbread for the Americans. I'm sure the others will do the same, once they hear about it."

"That will be lovely. I thank them all on behalf of the American forces." Elizabeth reached for the sugar tongs, carefully selected a sugar lump from the bowl, and dropped it in her tea. "I understand Mrs. Parsons's gingerbread is quite delectable."

Rita sniffed. "Some people seem to think so. Personally I prefer a rock cake. Something to sink one's teeth into."

"Quite," Elizabeth murmured. She stirred her tea and laid the spoon back in the saucer. "Speaking of Mrs. Parsons, she paid a visit to the house last evening. I believe she gave some of her gingerbread to Martin, in exchange for a packet of scented soap."

Rita looked dumbfounded. "I can't believe the nerve of that woman. Just because two of our members had been given the soap for the scavenger hunt, she takes it upon herself to march up to the Manor House and demand some, too. I have to tell you, your ladyship, that's not the sort of behavior I allow from our members of the Housewives League."

Exasperated by the woman's censure of a supposed friend, Elizabeth said mildly, "No harm done. It was, after all, a fair exchange. I'm quite sure Martin enjoyed the gingerbread, and in any case, Mrs. Parsons didn't want the soap for herself. She told Martin she wanted it for her granddaughter."

"Oh, yes. Pauline." Rita looked longingly at the Chelsea buns in front of Elizabeth. "I wonder what happened to her. She never comes down to see Maisie. You'd think she would since Maisie took her in when Pauline's mother died in that air raid. The child's father was killed at Dunkirk, you know."

Elizabeth disregarded Rita's obvious lust for a Chelsea bun. If she offered her one she was bound to take it and that would only delay her departure. "Oh, poor child. I know how it feels to lose one's parents."

"Well, it doesn't seem to have bothered her that much. Off she goes, back to London, with all that bombing going on, and never a word to Maisie. Or to our Lilly, for that matter."

Elizabeth looked at her in surprise. "Your daughter?"

Rita nodded. "Inseparable, they were. Took to

each other right away and went everywhere together. Then Pauline got herself mixed up with
a Yank. Gingerhead, he was. Hair the color of
carrots. After that our Lilly didn't see too much
of her. Then one day Pauline simply wasn't
there anymore. Gone to London, Maisie said.
Without one word to our Lilly."

Elizabeth stared at her. There was a nasty
feeling in the pit of her stomach. She wasn't
sure quite why at this point, but the sensation
was familiar. It had happened before. A strong
sense of knowing something important, yet unable to grasp just what it was.

"What's more, I don't know how Maisie can
send soap to her granddaughter," Rita added,
"when she doesn't even know where she's
living."

"I'm really not all that well acquainted with
Mrs. Parsons," Elizabeth said carefully. "Where
does she live?"

"Oh, she's not one of your tenants," Rita assured her. "She lives in one of the fisherman's
cottages down by the bay. Lovely garden, she
has. Always pottering about in it. I'll say that
much for her, she knows a lot about flowers.
Grows all kinds, she does."

"If you will excuse me, Rita," Elizabeth said
abruptly, "I have an important errand to run.
Do help yourself to a Chelsea bun." She left
Rita happily gobbling up the iced buns, and
hurried to her motorcycle.

It took her only a few minutes to wind her way

down the coast road to the bay. The cottages were scattered about the shoreline, but a friendly housewife directed her to Maisie Parsons's cottage. After parking her motorcycle out of sight around a curve in the lane, Elizabeth cautiously made her way to the cottage.

The front garden was a mass of flowers, everything from bright blue cornflowers and orange marigolds to white daisies and huge yellow sunflowers. Elizabeth's attention, however was centered on the shrubs bordering the confusion of blossoms. There had to be at least a half dozen bushes of daphne.

She was halfway back to the mansion when she finally pounced on what it was she was trying to remember. It was Martin, telling her and Violet how Maisie Parsons had insulted her own gingerbread. *She said that her gingerbread was moldy and should be disposed of as soon as possible.*

What if she hadn't said the word gingerbread at all, but instead had used Rita's version of a redhead.

Gingerhead.

Martin said he hadn't heard her clearly, because Sadie was talking to Joe Hanson at the time.

Elizabeth increased the speed of her motorcycle. Lieutenant Hanson had red hair. Maisie must have caught sight of him and Sadie in the hallway. Was she talking about disposing of her gingerbread, or the gingerhead? That certainly made a lot more sense.

231

Horrible, deadly sense.

Arriving back at the manor, she wheeled her motorcycle into the stables, then rushed around to the kitchen door. There was no time to wait for Martin's fumbled attempts to open the front door. She needed to talk to Sadie right away.

She found the housemaid in the kitchen, arguing with Violet, as usual.

"I told you I did dust him," Sadie declared, as Elizabeth burst through the door. "I remember rubbing his belly with me polishing cloth."

Violet swung around to face Elizabeth, her face creased in surprise. "Goodness, you're in a hurry. Is something wrong?"

"I hope not." Elizabeth fell on a chair, gasping for breath. "Sadie," she said, when she could speak clearly, "when you were in the Tudor Arms last night, did you happen to see any members of the Housewives League?"

"Yes, m'm, I did." Sadie looked puzzled. "Some of them were sitting near the piano. I remember thinking how daft they were to sit that close to a piano so they couldn't hear —"

"Sadie, forgive me for interrupting. Did you notice if one of the group was Maisie Parsons?"

"Oh, yes, m'm. She was there."

Elizabeth felt a spurt of fear. "Have you talked to Lieutenant Hanson since last night?"

Sadie's face lit up with her smile. "Yes, m'm. I seen him this morning. You'll never guess what he brought me." She reached in her pocket and pulled out what appeared to be a sheet of newspaper. "Look at this."

She thrust the paper at Elizabeth, who took it from her and smoothed it out. It was an article about Winston Churchill. There was a picture of him striding along some very familiar cliffs.

"I told everyone I seen Winnie, and nobody believed me," Sadie said, her voice rising in her excitement. "That's why Joe called me barmy last night. He didn't believe me neither. That's what made me cross with him so I walked out. Then this morning he brings me this piece of the newspaper and there it was. Full of apologies, he was."

She pointed a finger at the clipping in Elizabeth's hand. "Winston Churchill came down here on a secret mission. No one knows why. Some say it were his double made-up to look like him, so the spies would think he was here when he was really somewhere else. They're always trying to do him in, you know." She raised her chin and gave Violet a triumphant toss of her head. "See, I told you I seen him."

Violet clucked her tongue. "All right, missie, so you saw him. That doesn't mean you can skimp on your housework. You get up there and dust that suit-of-armor properly, like I told you to do."

Sadie slumped toward the door. "All right, I'm going." Then she paused. "Oh, wait, me newspaper story." She came back to the table and Elizabeth handed her the clipping.

233

"I'm going to keep it," she said, tucking it into her pocket. "It brought me and Joe together again." She grinned at Elizabeth. "He's taking me out again at the weekend."

"How nice." Elizabeth was genuinely happy for her. "I don't suppose Mrs. Parsons spoke to either of you last night?"

Sadie looked baffled. "It's funny you should say that. Joe gave her a lift home last night. She hurt her ankle. He's a really nice man, that Joe. He told me she gave him some gingerbread for helping her. He didn't want to take it, but she wouldn't let him leave without it." Sadie turned back to the door. "I hope he saves me a bit. I heard it was really yummy."

As the door swung behind her, Violet said testily, "Yummy? What kind of word is that? More of that American slang, I —" She broke off as Elizabeth flew across the room. "What's wrong with you?"

Elizabeth flung the words over her shoulder. "What did Martin do with that gingerbread?"

"He gave it to me. Said he didn't like ginger."

"Did you eat any of it?"

"Not yet, but —"

"Well, throw it out. I'll explain later. I have to ring the base." She didn't wait to hear Violet's answer. All she could do was pray that Joe hadn't yet sampled that gingerbread.

It took far too long for Earl to come to the telephone. When she finally heard his voice, she let out her breath in relief. "Oh, Earl, thank heavens you're there. I was so afraid you'd be out on a mission or something, and I have something to ask you that's desperately important."

His pause worried her. "How did you know?" he said at last.

Her heart sunk. Oh, God, no. Not Joe. "Is it Lieutenant Hanson?" she asked fearfully. "He's not dead, is he?"

Earl's voice sounded strange. "Joe? No, he's fine. At least, he was when he took off an hour ago. Why? Do you know something we don't?"

She gripped the handset and pressed it to her ear. "Last night Joe was given some gingerbread by one of our villagers. I need to know if he's eaten it yet, and if not, I want you to give it to your medics for testing. I think you'll find it contains poison."

"Gingerbread?" Earl sounded incredulous. "Are you sure?"

"No, I'm not at all sure. But we have to find out if I'm right before Lieutenant Hanson eats it. If I'm wrong I'll personally ask Maisie Parsons to replace it."

"Let's just hope he didn't take it with him." Earl hesitated. "I'll take care of it, and I'll call you back with the results."

"Thank you, Earl. I pray that I'm wrong, or at least that I rang you in time."

"Right." Again that odd pause, then he added, "I need to talk to you anyway. Soon. This evening?"

Her heart skipped. Now she remembered something else. Something he'd said when she first spoke to him. *How did you know?* She didn't like the way her stomach was jiggling.

Impatiently, she pushed her worries aside. That could wait until tonight. Right now the important thing was to find out if her hunch was right. "This evening," she agreed. "But you will ring me the minute you know about the gingerbread?"

"Promise. And Elizabeth?"

"Yes?"

"Don't do anything until you hear from me, all right?"

"I won't. I'll wait for you to ring me."

"Is that a promise?"

"I promise." She replaced the handset, and leaned back in her chair. How long would it take them to test the gingerbread? Had Joe Hanson already eaten some? He could be dying right now, somewhere over the Atlantic Ocean. All she could do was pray.

The telephone rang late that afternoon. Alone in her office, Elizabeth snatched up the phone. She'd sent Polly home earlier. The child had been drooping at her desk all morning, her red eyes and runny nose suggesting a summer cold was in the offing.

"Hello?" she said breathlessly. "This is the Manor House residence. You are speaking to Lady Elizabeth."

"Elizabeth."

As always, his voice caused her heart to leap with joy. "Earl! Did you find the gingerbread? Did you get it tested? Was I right?"

"Whoa, slow down there." He paused. "We found the tin of gingerbread. You were right, Elizabeth. It was loaded with enough poison to kill an elephant."

She hissed out her breath. "So the article in the book was right. Cooking doesn't kill the poison."

"Nope. It looks as if the lady crushed up the berries and mixed them into the gingerbread. It couldn't have tasted that good, but according to the lab techs, it wouldn't have taken more than a bite or two to kill a guy."

"What about Lieutenant Hanson?"

"Last report we had from his crate he's alive and well."

"Thank God." She felt weak with relief. "Then he must not have eaten any."

"Doesn't look like it."

"Thank you, Earl. I suppose now I should ring the constables."

"I guess so, though our guys have already gone to the lady's house. They'll be bringing her back here for questioning."

"When they do," Elizabeth said quietly, "ask them to find out what happened to her grand-daughter, Pauline."

It was late that evening when Earl finally tapped on the conservatory door. Elizabeth had spent the evening trying to work out the intricacies of the knitting pattern she'd bought, and had actually managed to complete several rows. She hastily tucked the work under the cushion of her wicker couch when she heard Earl's knock.

He looked grave when he came in, and again her stomach quivered with apprehension.

She waited while he poured himself a Scotch from the bottle she had ready for him and had settled himself in the rocker before saying a little impatiently, "Well, what happened? Is Maisie Parsons in custody? Did she admit to poisoning the gingerbread? Is Lieutenant Hanson still all right?"

Earl sipped his drink and put it down on the table between them. "Joe is fine. He arrived back from the mission safe and sound. Never touched the gingerbread. He was saving it for a midnight snack."

She nodded in relief. "And Mrs. Parsons?"

"They are holding her at the base until custody arrangements have been made with Scotland Yard."

Elizabeth drew a sharp breath. "So she did poison the gingerbread."

"Yes. She's responsible for the deaths of five young American servicemen."

Something in the way he said it touched her heart. "Oh, Earl, I'm so sorry. It must be devastating for you to lose them that way."

He reached for his glass again. "You hope and

pray that they'll make it back from a mission, and when they do you thank God. That's war. This . . ." He shook his head, momentarily speechless, then added, "This is something else. Such a terrible waste."

"I know." She put out a hand, leaning forward to touch him. "I truly am sorry."

He seemed lost in thought for a moment, then said more firmly, "Well, at least we stopped her from poisoning anyone else. Thanks to you. Who knows how many more young men would have lost their lives if it hadn't been for your persistence and intelligence. The United States Army Air Force owes you a great debt."

She didn't want anything from the USAAF. All she wanted was approval from him. "I'm just so very glad I could help." She was quiet with him for several moments, mulling over what had happened. Then, after watching him sip too fast at his drink, she added tentatively, "Did Mrs. Parsons tell the investigators why she killed those men?"

Sighing, he put down his glass. "Yes, she did. According to the report I received just before I left, Maisie Parsons confessed to the murders. Apparently, her granddaughter was in love with one of our guys here at the base. When she found out he was married, she slit her wrists. Maisie had seen them together, but all she knew about him was that he had red hair. Her granddaughter had refused to tell her anything else."

Now Elizabeth understood. "So she started

killing Americans with red hair, hoping eventually to get the right one."

Earl looked impressed. "Right! That's exactly what she did. Apparently she was frantic when her granddaughter died. She believes that suicide is a sin, and that it would prevent her granddaughter from entering heaven."

Elizabeth uttered a cry of dismay. "Oh, no. That poor woman."

"She was afraid she'd be blamed for the girl's death, since she was supposed to be taking care of her. So she hid the body. Our investigators found it early this evening, hidden in the coal shed beneath a pile of coal."

"That's enough to send someone out of her mind."

"I guess that's what happened." Earl reached for his drink again. "Something snapped, and she decided to go after the guy who was responsible. Unfortunately, all she knew was that he had red hair. It came down to eliminating all possible suspects."

Elizabeth shivered. "I wonder what will happen to her."

"I imagine she'll be put in an institution for the criminally insane."

"That's so sad."

"Yeah, it is sad."

She sent him a sharp glance, detecting something in his voice that worried her. "Earl, this must have been so unpleasant for you. Are you all right?"

He didn't answer her right away, worrying her further. Then he said quietly, "I'm afraid we still haven't caught up with the three guys who are causing all that trouble with our troops. Though at least, to our knowledge, they haven't killed anyone. It's more malicious mischief than anything."

"That's as may be. I still want them stopped." She studied his face, searching for some reassurance and finding none. "I suppose that's something we'll have to deal with now. And that goes for that doctor in North Horsham, too. I won't rest until they are all apprehended."

She watched him drain his glass and set it down. His expression suggested he had come to a decision of sorts, and now her faint trickle of dread became a torrent of fear. He had something to tell her. Something she wasn't going to like. She could see it in every line in his face, and in the way he held his body, as if bracing himself for an unpleasant task.

"What is it?" she said sharply. "What is it that you don't want to tell me?"

The infinite sadness in his eyes terrified her. "I never could keep anything from you, Elizabeth."

To her amazement and concern, he got up from the rocker and came over to sit by her side. He had never done that before, and now she was absolutely certain. This was the moment she had dreaded, ever since she realized that he'd stolen her heart.

She felt cold. So terribly, terribly cold. Every muscle in her face was clenched, and the hand he took in both of his trembled, in spite of her efforts to control it.

"Elizabeth," he said gently, "I do have something to tell you. My son has been in a car accident."

She smothered her cry of dismay as he continued speaking.

"He's in the hospital, in a coma. I've requested a transfer, and I'm leaving for the States in the morning."

Her throat closed up so tightly she had to force words through it. "Earl, I'm so dreadfully sorry. You know my heart and my prayers will go with you. Your family needs you now. I'm happy that you are able to join them. You know I wish with all my heart that your son makes a complete and speedy recovery."

He dropped his gaze, as if unable to meet hers. "I . . . don't know how long . . ."

"Or if ever," she finished for him. "I understand."

"No, I don't think you do." He got up abruptly and stood at the window, staring out at the dusk settling over the lawns and the distant trees.

She suddenly realized it was getting dark. She couldn't turn on the lamps until the blackout curtains had been drawn. She didn't want to turn on the lights. It was easier to deal with this terrible ache in her heart in the dark shadows of the quiet room.

One part of her prayed he would leave soon, before she broke down completely and made an utter, complete fool of herself. Another part of her prayed he would stay, because once he left, the agonizing chasm he left behind would be far too terrible to bear.

He wouldn't be able to help her judge the bake sale after all, she thought. It seemed an odd thing to fasten on, but somehow it seemed important. She'd been relying on him. How could she do it without him? How could she ever again enjoy anything without him?

She closed her eyes, and when she opened them again, he was standing before her. In spite of her misery, her heart leapt when he reached for her hand and gently pulled her to her feet.

"Elizabeth," he said, his deep voice resonating to the depths of her soul. "I want you to know that these last months have been among the happiest of my life."

She opened her mouth to answer him, but he laid a finger momentarily against her lips. "No, let me finish. You have made the worst times bearable, and the best times unforgettable. No one wants to be in a strange country fighting a war, but if there was ever a compensation, I got the very best when I met you. I want to thank you for making a soldier far from home feel welcomed, accepted, and privileged to be in your company."

Hardly able to speak, she prayed she could find the right words. These, she knew, might be the last words she ever spoke to him. She wanted, with all her heart, for them to mean enough to him that they would forever stay in his memory.

"I am the one who has been privileged," she told him. "You have brought so much joy into my life. I have learned so much from you, about your people, your lifestyle, your wonderful country. I've watched you fight many battles in your mind and your heart, and your compassion for your fellow man, your dedication to your duty, and your loyalty to your family has been a lesson and an inspiration. Thank you for making my world so bright in the midst of these terrible times."

She pulled in a deep breath, and was proud of the composure in her voice when she added, "I shall never forget you, Earl."

"Nor I you." He lifted her hands to his mouth and pressed his lips to each one. "Elizabeth, when this is over, I don't know if I'll be sent back here, or somewhere else. I just want you to know that wherever I go, I'll carry a part of you with me."

Her heart breaking, she pulled her hands from his grasp. "Just to make sure of that," she said unsteadily, "take this with you." She reached for the silk scarf she'd laid on the couch earlier. "An old-fashioned tradition, I know, but a good one."

He took the scarf from her and tucked it in his pocket. "I'll keep it with me always."

It was so dark now, she could barely see his face. Maybe it was just as well, she told herself. For to look in his eyes and see her pain reflected there would be too much.

He moved to the door, and she fought hard to keep the tears at bay. Unable to follow him, she just stood there, marking in her memory her very last sight of him.

He paused at the door, then turned to face her. "So long, Elizabeth. Stay out of trouble, all right?"

She clenched her jaw. "You, too." She could not say good-bye to him. That was too final. She could never say good-bye to him.

He turned to go, reaching for the door. Then, so suddenly it took her breath away, he spun around and took the three paces back to reach her.

His hands were rough on her arms as he pulled her toward him, but eagerly she welcomed them. His mouth found hers, and in a blaze of joy she clung to him, feverishly returning the long-awaited kiss.

It was over almost before she realized it was happening. With a muttered curse he let her go, strode to the door and was gone, leaving her dazed, aching and utterly, devastatingly alone.

We hope you have enjoyed this Large Print book. Other Thorndike, Wheeler or Chivers Press Large Print books are available at your library or directly from the publishers.

For more information about current and upcoming titles, please call or write, without obligation, to:

Publisher
Thorndike Press
295 Kennedy Memorial Drive
Waterville, ME   04901
Tel. (800) 223-1244

Or visit our Web site at:
www.gale.com/thorndike
www.gale.com/wheeler

OR

Chivers Large Print
published by BBC Audiobooks Ltd
St James House, The Square
Lower Bristol Road
Bath BA2 3SB
England
Tel. +44(0) 800 136919
email: bbcaudiobooks@bbc.co.uk
www.bbcaudiobooks.co.uk

All our Large Print titles are designed for easy reading, and all our books are made to last.